$9.95

D0923378

ALSO BY MALCOLM MacCLOUD

The Tera Beyond

A
GIFT OF
MIRRORVAX

A
GIFT OF
MIRRORVAX

MALCOLM MAC CLOUD

AN ARGO BOOK

ATHENEUM 1981 NEW YORK

Library of Congress Cataloging in Publication Data
MacCloud, Malcolm.
A gift of Mirrorvax.

"An Argo book."
Summary: Owned by the planet Vax's largest
corporation, Michael is sent on a secret mission to
a shadow world, where he is totally unprepared for
the adventures awaiting him.
[1. Science fiction] I. Title.
PZ7.M13364Gi   [Fic]   81-1399
ISBN 0-689-30849-3   AACR2

For *Robert*, as a fable
and
For *Emily*, as a tribute

FOREWORD

Because much of this story takes place on Vax, a distant planet, use of some words is uncustomary. The following list will help clarify unusual Vaxan terminology.

advocate   a Vaxan lawyer
air-shuttle   Transvax-built hovercraft
artillery   lasar-based weaponry
asset   a purchased resource
auction complex   where Conglomerates purchase resource
barb-thrower   the Syntac weapon
capital   breeders bought by the Government
child-bearing suburbs   where children are born and raised
chrona   the Vaxan year; monetary unit based on a year's work of one worker
coil   *see* death-coil
Conglomerate   one of the three great corporations of Vax; Transvax, Syntac, or Medron
death-coil   the Transvax weapon
Government stock   workers owned by the Government
Medron   a Conglomerate specializing in medical supplies and housing
province   one of the five territorial divisions of Vax

recyclage   a slang term for a person who is resold
resource   an untrained or unpurchased person
resource suburb   a training center for resource
Secretariat   the governing council of a Conglomerate
Space Operations Corporation   a division of Transvax concerned with space exploration and travel
Statutes   the constitution of Vax
suburb   a working unit of one million people
Syntac   a Conglomerate specializing in food and fabric synthesis
Transvax   a Conglomerate controlling Vaxan communications and transportation.
Tribunal   a Vaxan court, on a province or world level
tube transport   Transvax underground transportation
venom-eggs   the Medron weapon

CONTENTS

PART
1

AUCTION DAY

HE HAD COME to an auction complex before, and this one seemed identical to the one in Valacar. It had the same menacing look when seen from an air-shuttle—a stark aluminum tetrahedron with cement concourses like tentacles running out from it, packed with people. And once he joined the crowd, he found this auction complex had the same instruction signs he remembered seeing that day in Valacar; and the same long, domed corridors inside, carpeted with people and sprinkled with drops of light from high plastic windows. The place even sounded and smelled the same as Valacar had. A machinery-like murmur hummed in the crowd, and in spite of newly processed white resource robes on almost everyone, the corridors smelled vaguely of thick breath and of sweat.

But, he realized with a deepening frown, not everything was the same. Catching sight of his blurred reflection in the aluminum panel on the nearest wall, he saw that his dark green robe stood out in the sea of white around him. He felt the eyes of the resource on him, and he reddened as he imagined he could hear them muttering, "Recyclage," or laughing silently into their hands.

Putting his hands to his throat, he wanted to rip the robe

3

and cast it off. But his shame ebbed, and he pretended he had raised his hands to straighten his collar. He forced a smile. *Recyclage* was not such a bad word as he had always thought, perhaps; it meant only that he had earned a second chance to be bought by one of the three great Conglomerates. They will stop laughing, he thought, staring at the resource, when I became an advocate for Transvax or Syntac or Medron. And some of them will stop laughing when the Government computer has to buy them because the Conglomerate computers will not bid.

They had not bid for him on his first auction day.

The humiliation of that day stung his cheeks still as he thought of it. It glared at him, green-eyed, when he looked at his robe. He remembered still lowering himself into the auction chair, looking wildly between the four computers as each spelled out his name. Something in his stomach twitched as he remembered looking from screen to screen to find each staring, blank, empty, undisturbed, until finally the government computer had offered only a single digit for him—he could not remember the exact number—and men in green robes had come and taken him, stunned, into the government preparation room. That had been three chronas ago, three orbits of the world Vax around its sun. And now, coming to an auction complex again, he was that much older than the resource crowding around him.

He was slightly taller than most of them, so he could see over the sea of heads and knew that the corridor narrowed ahead. It diverged; block-letter signs told them to make four single-file lines on ramps that led in different directions. He did not jostle with the others for a place as he had done the first time. But soon he found himself between a young-looking girl and a brawny boy on a ramp that first led up, then dipped and twisted through a doorway. His first ramp, too, had led upward.

He looked away toward another ramp that spiraled toward an opening in the ceiling. He thought he saw a colored robe among the white, but before he could be sure, his ramp passed into an aluminum-walled passageway. Turning into it, he found that the girl ahead of him had turned around and was staring at his robe.

He glared at the floor, pretending he had not noticed her. But she spoke. "Excuse me," she said. "Do you mind if I ask you something?"

She had a high-pitched voice, and when he looked at her, he was sure she was too young to be auctioned. Her face was slim and sharp, her hair abnormally long, and her eyes wide and green and wild like an animal's. "No," he said, folding his arms. "I don't mind."

"Are you . . ." she said, "I mean, *were* you . . . capital?"

He felt himself turning red. "No," he said. "No. I was in training in Conglomerate law. In another chrona I would have been an advocate."

"Oh." She sighed. "I'm sorry for the mistake, but when I saw your green robe, I couldn't help but wonder. And the reason I asked you," she said quickly, seeming to understand his grimace, "is not because you look particularly like capital, but because I rather hope I end up as capital myself. I would like that best."

He hid his amazement in a frown. "Someone has to be capital if we are to have more resource," he said blandly. "And the child-bearing suburbs are satisfactory, from what I have heard."

"I helped in a child-bearing suburb during my resource training," the girl answered. "You would be surprised to find out what pleasant places they are. I don't see why people look down on them so. In the old days, before the Conglomerates, almost everybody was capital, and even though they say it was less efficient, it must have been pleasant . . ."

Glancing beyond her, he stopped listening. She indeed would be perfect for a child-bearing suburb with such outdated notions and self-fabricated emotions. He gritted his teeth when he remembered she had thought he was capital.

5

Cold air from the grill above him did little to cool the heat that built up in his cheeks. The girl, seeing his disinterest, stopped herself short and turned around. The line was moving more quickly now, though still they only shuffled along.

"The government doesn't train many resource to be advocates," the girl said after a time. "Why do they want to resell you?"

He shifted his weight to his other leg and folded his arms. "I don't know," he said, his voice pinched. "This morning I received an order—through the computer—to report here. I don't know why."

"Maybe one of the Conglomerates wants you as an advocate," she said.

"But I am not an advocate yet," he said. "I don't think it could be that . . ." He faltered, for this was the only real hope he had about being resold. It was of course quite impossible that a Conglomerate would want a partially trained advocate, but in the confused hours since he had received the computer command, he had pushed himself into half believing it to be the reason he had been called here.

Ahead of him the girl touched the wall with her fingertips and pretended to look at her smeared reflection. Her body as well as her face was thin, and her arms were lost in the long white sleeves. The quiet curve of her lips and the subdued glitter in her eyes were disconcerting when she slowly turned toward him and lifted her eyes to his. A movement in the line jostled them ahead and broke the contact between them, but the girl turned to him again and asked him what his name was.

He paused, then gave her his identification number.

"I mean," she said, "what is your *real* name?"

"Michael," he said crisply. His own name sounded odd to him.

"That is a pleasant name. Do you know where you got it?"
He shrugged.

"The Government assigns you a number once you leave the child-bearing suburb and are taken to the resource suburb. But your first name, your real name, has nothing to do with computers or filing systems. It is the name your parents gave you. Think of that." She paused. "The name my parents gave me was Catherine—"

"Look up ahead," he said, reaching over her shoulder to point. "The corridor is going to branch onto the auction ramps. We are almost to the auction chambers. I know; I have been through this before. Maybe . . . maybe we shouldn't talk anymore." The girl turned away when he said this, and he felt a twinge. But he knew he could not have tolerated more of her bubble-headed prattle about names and child-bearing suburbs and parents, not when his whole future would be decided in only a few minutes.

When at the junction of ways the girl went to the left, he turned to the right. He wondered, suddenly, whether she would get her wish, whether the Government computer would buy her as capital. He somehow hoped so, since she seemed to want it so badly. And chances were good she would if she had been trained in a child-bearing suburb. The computers, after all, screened the full files of a resource before the auction began.

The Conglomerate computers would know he was being auctioned as recycle. He felt his shoulders tighten; the computers would know he was being resold, and that would make them bid fewer chronas for him. Perhaps none of the computers would bid at all, and again the Government computer—by Vaxan law—would have to offer some menial price for him.

Perhaps ten people ahead, the door to the auction chamber stood out, a dark frame against the play of light and color beyond. Michael heard the computers clicking, humming, chattering, muttering to themselves. The different pitches of their sounds made the interplay of machinery sound like a hurried conversation. An argument perhaps. Or, to be more accurate, bidding. The noise, accompanied by shifts of light, continued for some time. Finally, one by one, the various pitches of clicks stopped, leaving a low rattling sound, which was accompanied by a predominance of blue light in the chamber door. Whoever had been in the auction seat had been bought by Transvax, the richest of the Great Conglomerates; and from the duration of the bidding, he had probably gone for a high price.

Transvax, Michael thought. As a resource he had always dreamed of being bought by Transvax, the corporation that controlled the world's travel and communications. For Transvax, though it had fewer assets than Syntac and a smaller chrona pool than Medron, was by far the most powerful Vaxan Conglomerate. Its advocates always won their suits in the Tribunal, and its projected expansion into space exploration and travel made it the fastest growing corporation of the three.

He stopped himself from thinking further. He must not get his hopes up; hope would only hurt him that much more if he was rebought by the government. He narrowed his eyes at the opening into the auction chamber, now only half a dozen people away. He should not delude himself about what might happen. Transvax, after all, bought fewer resource—and doubtlessly fewer recyclage—than either of the other Conglomerates.

As he saw more of the auction chamber, more memories of his first auction came back. The old humiliation returned to make his arms prickle, just as they had when the Government men had led him from the auction chamber in Valacar three chronas ago. Suddenly he became fierce; pride and indignation swelled his chest and made his fingers redden as he hooked them in his belt. "I am better than recyclage," something inside him seemed to shout, "and better than Government stock." He raised his chin and shook back his dark hair. He felt the computer lights from the auction chamber throw odd stripes of light across his face. His lips twisted into a snarl. He told himself silently, promised himself, that he would not be bought by the Government again. A Conglomerate computer would take him: Medron, Syn-

8

tac, or perhaps even Transvax. And if any of them did, he would show them what he was worth. He would make them pleased that they had bought him.

Before long the man in front of him moved through the door and took a seat in the center of the room. Michael, standing in the doorway, saw all of the auction chamber: the four computers, each with curving panels dancing with lights and a great screen like a single, monstrous eye. The Government computer, on the far side of the room, was the smallest of the four; its screen was tiny, greenish, and flickering. The other three computers, towering cylinders of steel, were almost identical, except that above each broad, pulsing screen was a different insignia: the gold shield for Medron, the red-rimmed semicircles of Syntac, and the silver triangle of Transvax trailing an exhaust of blue fire.

"Transvax," Michael whispered, knotting his fingers together. "It will be Transvax."

The man who had just taken the auction seat seemed paralyzed there. The color in his face drained away when the sounds of machinery began. When the overhead lights went dim, he hunched down in the chair, clutching his arms, glancing fearfully from screen to screen. All, except for a printout of his name, remained blank and unblinking. Finally, after a single digit from the Medron computer, lights began to flash. The chatter of circuitry heightened until with an explosion of light from the Medron computer and a shrill sonette from the Government console, the overhead lights returned to their former brightness to reveal the buyer and the price on a high, silver screen. MEDRON: 82.2 chronas. Michael narrowed his eyes as the gold-robed attendants helped the now-grinning man from his chair. Eighty chronas was greater than the duration of work Medron might expect to get from the man; the computer, it seemed, had far overbid. Which would mean that this computer bank would be more conservative for the next few rounds to come. The bidding would be quieter without an aggressive third party, especially when recycle was up for sale. Michael tried to swallow, but he found his throat too dry.

When the lights had fully brightened, he knew it was his turn.

Holding his head high, he strode across the floor, and glancing between computers, he sat down in the seat in the middle of the room. The computers were nearly silent now; their lower lights pulsing only slowly; their screens blank, waiting; the click of their motorworks faint and preparatory. As Michael centered his back in the cushion, he saw that there were faint marks on the arms of the chair where other fingers had curled around them. The air smelled slightly of machines, of oil and circuits and heat, but more strongly of something like acid that Michael dared not identify. The girl he had met in the passage might have called it fear, but Michael, as he faced the four sightless screens, was not afraid. Fear, after all, was nowadays only a vocabulary word on resource training screens. No one in the ordered world of Vax would be afraid. No one in the ordered world of Vax *could* be afraid. There was no reason for fear. But fear—the word that ought to have been abstract and foreign to him—kept repeating itself in his mind and in the drum of his fingers.

"Transvax," he muttered to himself. "It will be Transvax."

The lights had begun to dim, but none of the computers seemed to be making more noise. The Syntac screen flashed once, but because of a momentary power fluctuation, it seemed; for no digits appeared beneath Michael's name, and the other computers remained quiet. The light grew so dim that Michael could see his hands, clawed on the ends of the chair arms, only as blurs. The breathless silence intensified, and he swung his head involuntarily toward the Government computer. A large red light began to flash beside the screen, as he remembered it had on the day he was first sold.

A sudden hiss of motorworks and a flood of light snapped

his head toward the Transvax computer. But he had not time to read the bid before a second flash from the Syntac computer countered. Then an answering growl from the Medron computer with an accompanying plume of gold light from its screen, in which the figure 95 caught in his mind. The Medron computer, he just had time to think, must have a short circuit. But before he had a chance to reread the figure, it had already changed, in answer to the Transvax computer, to 115. He swung around to look at the Transvax screen, but a 135 leaped at him from the Syntac computer, which, after an indignant roar of machinery from the Transvax computer, changed to 145.

At that point Michael decided he must be dreaming. The highest price that had been paid for anyone he knew was just less than a hundred chronas, and then only for a fully trained technician with experience in Conglomerate law. Bids as he had just seen—or imagined he had seen—were totally unprecedented; therefore his mind, in his dream, had far surpassed any realm of reality. He should have recognized it was all a dream, he thought, reassured, when he had first received the summons to the auction complex. Law students in governmental education suburbs were not resold. His dream was simply a retracing of the past—the painful moment of his first auction. His mind was trying to change what had happened.

He would wake up, he was sure, all too soon. Until he did, he might as well enjoy it. Lounging back in the chair, he smiled at the absurdity of it all. Staring at his legs, he watched bursts of light recolor his robe. A stab of blue light, then a tongue of red light following, then a glimmering path of blue again that was suddenly turned green by a square of gold, then orange with the added light from the Syntac computer. It all reminded him of fireworks he had seen once while visiting the Syntac regional headquarters in Valacar, only this performance was set to a symphony of angry machinery whose roar made his ears buzz. He clapped his hands to the sides of his head. Glancing up, he saw a four-digit number glitter on the Syntac screen, then disappear with a din of machinery from his left and a sharp buzz from the Government computer. The lights above began to brighten, but their glow was stained with blue.

Shielding his eyes with his hands, he peered at the Transvax screen. He read the number below his name, quelled, then squinted and read the digits several times, muttering them to himself. "Two thousand chronas," he heard himself say. The echo of his voice reached his mind distorted, odd-sounding as though in some foreign language. He sank back into the chair and closed his eyes; opening them, he reread the screen. The impossible amount remained. And as the numbers sparkled on the high screen, he heard murmuring, from both people and machinery, growing around him.

Staring still at the Transvax screen, he tried to stand up. But his knees would not take him from the chair, and when he pushed up with his arms, his elbows buckled. *Two thousand chronas!* he thought fiercely. Reason told him such a bid could be given only in a dream. But if this was a dream, it was a starkly real one: the odd weight of his body cupped in the chair, the odd tingling in his throat, the rapidly flashing warning lights on the Government computer, and the number of robed attendants who hurried from half-hidden doors beside the computers told him he was not dreaming.

The first men to rush into the auction chamber were green-robed Government retainers who wore badges of the auction complex police and who stared in disbelief at the figure on the Transvax screen, then at Michael. From behind the Medron computers came gold-robed attendants; they gaped at Michael, blinking in the light, hunching in their robes.

But the two Syntac men who appeared a moment later wore faces like robots'. They came slowly and moved only a few paces into the room. Something about their calmness drew attention toward them, toward their pressed lips, toward their glittering eyes, toward gleaming metal objects in their red-gloved hands. The taller of the two raised his arm, and with it the barrel of a pistol. He motioned to four more armed Syntac men, who emerged behind him, into positions around the room, circling Michael.

"No one will move," he said stonily, nodding at the auction-complex police. "There has been a misunderstanding here. Syntac will take the resource." Michael opened his mouth, but not even breath came out.

With a sudden explosion of footfalls, blue-robed men burst through another door and fanned out into the room. Most of them flung steel coils at isolated Syntac guards; Michael saw one crumple to the floor, the serpentile cord around his arms and throat. Shouting began. Something hissed through the air above him. A coil flashed over his head. He saw a blue-robed Transvax man drop, clutching his shoulder. He saw the Government police backing toward their computer. He heard one of the computers start a siren.

A Transvax man reached him first. He seized Michael's arm and dragged him to his feet. "Come with me!" he shouted. "Quickly!"

But Michael's foot caught on the auction chair, and he fell. Before the Transvax man could pull him to his feet, something whispered above his shoulder and caught in the padding of the chair. He stared at it for a moment before he realized it was a barb, a many-pronged hook of poisoned steel. He saw that one of the first two Syntac men lay paralyzed in a steel coil; the second one, however, still had in his hand a barb-thrower. He slowly steadied it on Michael.

COIL
AND DAGGER

MICHAEL SPRANG to his feet and ran, but before he and the Transvax man had gone halfway to the door, the man's grip on Michael's arm went heavy, and dragging against Michael, he fell slowly to the floor, a silver barb in his shoulder like a burr. Michael stopped and knelt, trying to support him, but another Transvax man tore him away, and together with two others pushed him through the doorway. Michael sprawled forward onto the floor and heard the shouting die away as the computer closed the door behind them.

The four remaining Transvax men, once the door had shut, hooked their coils back at their sides and clumped around Michael. Their faces were pale and their lips red with exertion. Two of them helped Michael to his feet while the two others, shouting something to each other, moved to a control console, dumped themselves in chairs, and began pushing buttons. One remained beside Michael, and the other went to the door and peered through a slit-shaped aperture in it.

"What does it look like?" a tall man at the control panel demanded.

"It's swarming with greenrobes now, but otherwise things are clear. Syntac has retreated, at least for the moment

14

Can't tell much more."

"We can't hold the door forever," the man beside Michael said.

"Not if the greenrobes order us to open it," the man by the door said.

Michael rubbed his arms lightly. "What on Vax is going on here?" he managed to blurt out. "I don't understand why . . . why all this is happening!"

"You don't have to understand. Especially not now," the man beside Michael said, looking at him squarely. "If you are worth any of the money Transvax just bid for you, keep your mouth shut. Cooperate until we can get you out of danger. What's happening with Syntac now?"

The man by the door squinted, then grunted. "Can't be sure. But it looks quiet."

"It won't be for long," the man beside Michael snapped. "They've committed themselves now. They've defied the Statutes. Their next move will be an attack on us here. They won't let us get our resource out of the complex alive, if they can help it."

Michael opened his mouth but closed it again when the man beside him, whom he guessed to be the auction complex commander, glared at him. Peeling off black gloves, the commander moved to the control board, where he bent over a screen. "Any directives from the Secretariat?"

"Not since the first one, sir." The man reached for a far button and jabbed it, a frown growing on his face. "I think one is trying to come through, but the Syntac computer must be jamming it!"

"Switch to another channel, then. We have got to have orders from the Secretariat, or we can't move this resource from this room—"

"We may have to, sir," the man at the door broke in, his face again pale. "Things are beginning to look grim out there."

"What do you mean?"

"The greenrobes," he said, "are withdrawing. I think

they'll try to seal off this auction chamber. But something is happening near the Syntac computer." He craned his neck, as if to get a better view of something. "I saw movement over there."

The commander set his teeth and hooked his fingers in his beard. "Justin," he said in a strained voice, "we need that message."

"I can't get it, sir," the man said, hunching over the panel, his fingers playing over the keyboards. "Syntac must have known about this for almost as long as we have. I thought first they were just interfering with our circuits locally, but they seem to be jamming the air frequencies between here and Helcar. It's hard to believe, but I think they're using their satellite . . . they seem to want to get hold of that resource pretty badly—"

"Their satellite?" Michael muttered.

"Transvax wants him, too," the commander growled, "and if we fall through, we won't have a good time of it with the Secretariat—if we survive, that is. There must be something you can do to bypass the air frequencies. There has to be."

The man at the console looked up, wrinkles of frustration patterning his forehead. "I can't fight the Syntac satellite, so there isn't anything I can do to get through to Helcar—unless . . . well, I might patch a connection through the underground cables, but that will take time."

"Do it," the commander snapped. "And do it fast—"

"The last of the greenrobes are gone now, sir," the man at the door said. "They've turned out the lights, and I can't see a blasted thing!"

"Syntac will make their move any minute," the commander said grimly. "Syntac can't afford to wait until the Government brings in their Conglomerate Control people. Blast it, man, do you have anything yet? And Martin, has the computer secured the escape passages?"

"At least as far down as ground level," the other man at the console answered.

The commander glanced at the door at the back of the control room, then at Michael. "We may have to make a run for it, but I don't want to leave here yet. Not until we have orders from the Secretariat. I don't know where they want us to take this resource—"

"I see something!" the man at the door said. "I saw a flash."

"Something is starting to come through the underground," the man at the console said, biting his lip. "But it's coming bit by bit."

"Great Transvax!" the man by the door shouted. "It's artillery!"

Though Michael had no idea what kind of artillery it was, he, too, had seen the flash in the crack at the edge of the door, and by the movement of the commander's jaw beneath his beard, he guessed it must be formidable. The gnawing hollowness in his stomach grew deeper and sharper, and he began to back slowly toward the rear door when he saw the crack go bright twice more.

A high-pitched moaning began. At first barely detectable beneath the chattering of the Transvax computer, it grew louder and deeper; then it became shrill, and the auction chamber door seemed to vibrate. The guard at the door threw his hands over his ears; the commander bent further over the console, wincing; and Michael, staring at the slit in the door saw a light pulsing there that grew brighter and redder with the escalation of the moaning sound.

"Blast it!" the man at the door shrieked. "We've got to get that resource out of here!"

"Keep calm!" the commander shouted back. Michael could hardly hear him because of the noise, now a throbbing roar. "Our orders from the Secretariat are coming through now." He hunched down, his eyes darting over a screen Michael could not see. "We are to deliver this resource—alive at all costs—to . . ." The commander went on, but Michael heard nothing, for the pitch of the roar heightened, and with a tremendous burst of sparks from the computer console, the lights on the control boards and those above him went out.

Faint fire sparkled on the control boards for an instant, floodlighting terror on the commander's face. The darkness closed in, thick and smelling of overheated metal, and from somewhere beyond the far-removed crackle of circuitry, the waiting sound began to escalate again.

"They've hit the computer!" the commander shouted. The harshness of his voice told Michael he had expected nothing so drastic. "Their next bolt will down the door. We've got to make a run for it." The four men blundered into the darkness to Michael; he could see nothing, but he sensed their tension and heard them breathing heavily as they jostled him across a dark threshold into a dark corridor. A light glowed at the far end.

Behind them artillery howled, and red lightning lit the aperture of the door. "Run for it!" the commander shouted. "Don't stop running till you get to the concourse."

Stumbling at first in the near darkness, they began to run, two in front of Michael, two behind. The skirts of their robes hobbled their strides. Their breathing and footfalls echoed thunderously but did not mask the rising scream from the auction chamber. Before they reached the end of the corridor, a bolt of light struck at their backs, and sparks sputtered from the door of the computer room.

"Run!" the commander coughed. "Run!"

They burst into light, into a high aluminum vault crisscrossed with stairs and walkways, flanked with wide doors. Blue-robed men emerged from two of the doors carrying long mirrorlike shields on their arms and Transvax death coils looped around their shoulders. They clumped around Michael's group, but some of them moved past and started into the corridor. The commander, between fits of coughing, shouted something to another bearded man about being late with backup support. The other man yelled in return that he had had to hold off a Syntac attack against another portal and had come as fast as he could. "By Trans-

18

vax!" the commander sputtered, when he heard this. "Syntac's smashed Conglomerate law this time! We'll bring them to the Tribunal for this—they've jammed our air contact with Helcar—and they're using artillery."

"We thought they might," the other man growled. "We're more prepared than you give us credit for. We'll take care of Syntac and their artillery. You worry about your job, getting *him*"—the man threw a hand at Michael—"out of here."

"The passages to the shuttleport," the commander said, "are they clear?"

"They were a few minutes ago, but Syntac has mobilized. They may give you trouble out on top."

The commander nodded and seized Michael's arm. Motioning to his men, he dragged Michael to a spiral stairway and shoved him up the first flight of steps. Michael gripped the rail for support and saw out of the corner of his eye the Transvax guards pouring into the corridor. But the commander shouted for him to run, so he hurried up the steps, then jogged along the ramp. Footfalls pounded mechanically behind him, as if he would be trampled if he dared slow down. The ramp plunged into a dimly lit tunnel. The commander goaded him on with a fist in his back. But in spite of a shout behind, Michael slowed then stopped when the corridor made a turn.

For fire spurted, red and glittering like fireworks, at the far end of the passage, and a haze of metallic smoke hung beneath flickering light-panels. The commander, shoving Michael behind him, cursed. "They've hit the shuttleport, too. The filthy redrobes! And they have artillery there, too, by the look of it. No use getting ourselves caught in that." Muttering, the commander ripped black gloves from his belt, pulled them on, then took a death-coil from his shoulder. "We may be in for a fight wherever we go, but let's try for the tubes. Syntac can't have penetrated that far down yet." He turned the coil in his hand, flexing it. "But Syntac has gone far this time. We've got to expect everything."

With Michael held in their circle, they started off again, not running this time only walking swiftly, their robes hissing against the metal of the floor. The commander guided them through dizzying mazes of passages, down lightless stairs, through machinery-filled rooms, in and out of shallow-shafted elevators. Michael lost all sense of direction and knew only that they were progressing downward. He soon guessed that they had dropped far below ground level—he sensed how deep they were by the subdued glimmer of lights, by the thickness of the air, by the booming their steps made. He heard more echoing sounds, very distant—screams of sirens and wails of artillery—but he no longer paid attention to them, even when they sounded near and the commander, gritting his teeth, took a passage leading away from them. Instead Michael limited his thoughts to the circle of men around him, to the play of light on the coils clenched in their fists, and to the odd glitter in their eyes when they looked at him. He dared think of no more.

He was sure, soon, that what the commander had meant by the tubes was the Transvax underground transport system. Which meant, seemingly, that they meant to take him somewhere within the city of Medracar or at least in the province of Vaxa Meda, for so far as he knew, the tube transport systems did not extend farther. When people traveled to cities in other provinces, they took Transvax air-shuttles. Yet the commander had intended to take him to the air-shuttles at first, so perhaps— He stopped himself, noticing muted shouting from somewhere above.

Finally they came to a long, high-roofed room lit by vague clumps of fluorescent lights overhead. A thick hump of concrete ran through its center like a half-submerged pipe. A gap in the hump halfway between the walls revealed an aluminum cylinder, a sub-transport unit similar to those Michael had often ridden between suburbs, but much smaller. The lights glittered on its shell, and as they approached, Michael saw that the blue triangle of Transvax gleamed on its door. He realized at once that the transport was not at all what he had anticipated.

One of the Transvax men hooped his coil on his shoulders, took off his gloves, wedged them under his arm, then punched a code into a console beside the gap in the tube. The doors of the transport unit slid back; peering in, Michael saw only two seats, both heavily padded.

"Where are you taking me?" Michael demanded, moving away from the door. "I want to know what you are planning to do with me."

The commander scowled and pretended not to hear Michael's question. "I hope you know the code for Tandra," the commander said to the man at the console. "It's in Hedris province—"

"Tandra!" Michael interrupted. "Why are you taking me there?"

"We're not *taking* you, to begin with," the commander said coolly. "We're *sending* you. That's our order. And our order didn't give a reason, no more than the Secretariat gave our computer bank a reason for bidding two thousand chronas for you. If you're smart, boy, you'll wait for answers and not ask questions. They're bound to be upset about what's happened here when you get to the other end, so I wouldn't irritate them with any questions, if I were you. Get in."

Michael hesitated. The commander's eyes narrowed until they were only blue slits, and he fingered his coil, passing it restlessly through his gloves. But a sudden sound made his head snap away; footballs drummed from the corridor outside, growing swifter and louder as half a dozen red-robed men burst from the far door, barb-throwers upraised.

"Get in, fool!" the commander shouted; his voice throbbed against the high ceiling. Michael ducked through the doorway, and only a split second later, the doors lurched closed, leaving him in darkness. He stumbled into one of the seats and fastened himself in it blindly, breathing gustily. Something pinged against the shell of the transport. He heard shouting, faint and haunting, almost like whisperings of machinery. But he felt no tremor of movement; the unit remained doggedly fixed. Something heavy fell against the wall of the unit, and something else slapped against the door.

What if the Syntac men brought down all the Transvax men before they could send the unit on its way? It would then be only a matter of time before the Syntac men found the code to open the door or destroy the unit with artillery. He shuddered at the thought and slid deeper into the seat. He no longer heard shouting, and he thought he heard buttons being pushed—carefully and haltingly—on the console outside.

He closed his hand over his eyes when the inner cabin lights came on. The doors shuddered, and for a horrifying second, he thought they would open, but instead a low-pitched humming began, like the sound the artillery had made, but deeper. As the sound grew louder, the transport began to vibrate, then to shake; then, without warning, it jerked forward, throwing Michael's head against the cushioning of his seat. The unit accelerated rapidly. It drove the breath from Michael's body and teased tears from his eyes until, after a final jolt forward, it reached smooth forward momentum.

For a long time he just sat, gripping his arm rests, sensing the vibration of the unit's movement. He was free, he thought. He had escaped. He was alive. But for what—to what end? What would happen next, when the tube transport stopped? After his recent experience, he had no idea of what might meet him in Tandra.

Tandra, he thought, lowering his eyebrows. Tandra was not the seat of the Transvax Secretariat. He had heard something about Transvax in Tandra before, but the relationship between the two eluded him.

Tandra was a province on the other side of the world. The thought chilled him, and it made him think of the Syntac satellite that had blocked Transvax communication.

How powerful these Conglomerates were, to claw at one another in space! The arm of Transvax was strong, too; with him in its grip it was receding toward Tandra and toward whatever waited for him there.

"I won't bother them with questions," he said aloud to himself, remembering what the commander had said. But the commander, he realized suddenly, might be dead. The thought made him remember the smell of burning electronics and the feel on his arm of the man who had fallen in the auction chamber.

To take his thoughts from the pictures flashing in his mind, he began to explore the interior of the transport. There was little more than the curved metal ceiling, the padded seats, and a plastic cabinet that reminded him of the one over the sink in his cubicle. Opening it, he found that it was packed with cans, tins, and plastic-covered packages. He fished out one of the tins. He flinched a little when he saw the Syntac emblem stamped into the aluminum. This was Syntac A5, an energy food. He opened it and ate, but his mouth was so dry he could scarcely taste it, so he found a can of Syntac-bottled water and drank until he could finish the food. He toyed with a few more of the tins, grimacing at each Syntac label until he came to something in a yellow plastic tube. Tranquilizers. Medron tranquilizers. He opened the tube, knocked a tablet into his hand, and swallowed it with a gulp of water. Then he closed the cabinet and reclined into his seat. He pressed his eyes shut.

Only this morning his life had been an ordered routine of sleeping, eating, and studying. Only this morning he had buried his head in his blankets when he had heard the waking siren. He had sat on the edge of his bed for a long time, staring at the floor, wondering how he could face another grinding day. He had dangled small rewards—a promise of an extra bit of food that evening, an extra moment of self-determined reading at the library—all to make himself begin his work. But his schedule had hardly begun when he had received the message.

And now his old, familiar routine, the thing he had both hated and needed most, lay behind him in the advocate training complex. Something told him that what lay ahead would not be as pleasant and secure. But it would engulf him and make him part of it. Part of Transvax, the greatest of the Great Conglomerates. And he would be an efficient part of it, too; he had no doubt of that. For what Transvax had paid for him in chronas and lives, he had to give adequate return. He would do for them whatever they asked of him.

The steady movement of the transport and the hum of the lights made him drowsy. Or was that the tranquilizer he had taken? Or had he taken a tranquilizer at all? He suddenly could not remember. He could remember nothing but cradling his head in the seat, folding his arms comfortably, and letting the last spark of recollection die away.

He did not dream. Not exactly. But he saw on his eyelids the thin girl he had met in the auction complex; only now she wore green, as he had, and she was smiling. Looking down, he saw himself in Transvax blue and laughed at her. She began to cry, and he laughed at her again. But when he looked down again, he realized the blue he had seen was not a robe; instead it was a great gloved hand that gripped him. He cried out to the girl, to have her help him free himself. But he saw nothing more than blackness and a distant glimmer, crescent-shaped, of green.

THE ARM
OF TRANSVAX

"OF COURSE," a voice said in the blackness, "we will take all of this to the Tribunal. Our advocates, in fact, have already filed a case at Medracar, and the Conglomerate Control people have agreed to fine the Syntac Secretariat immediately and constrict their asset-build-up in Vaxa Meda province. We will have no trouble making our suit good, I'm told, and we are bound to recover our losses at Medracar within the chrona. Oh, yes. The damage was considerable. Record-breaking, they say. But not irreversible, no. Not by any means, not now that we have collected the resource here. Yes, he's here. In my office, at present. No. Unconscious. It seems they tranquilized him before sending him. No, I don't know why. As I said, we have had no contact with the Medracar auction complex since we sent the Secretariat's order through. Naturally I don't mind. He is your department's asset, after all. He has been duly processed. Oh, I don't know that. But if he hasn't awakened by the time you come over, I can have one of my assistants give him a stimulant. Very well, then. By that time I'll have him awake and waiting for you . . ."

Michael, swimming away from drowsiness, opened his eyes. Light from broad windows stung them, but turning his head away, he found that he was lying on a sofa with his head propped up with cushions. One of his legs dangled over the edge, and his toes brushed against the carpet. He looked at the windows again and saw buildings beyond them and a semi-circular desk near them, where a plump man in a blue robe was staring at a screen affixed to a silver pillar. "I assure you again, sir, that he is in fine condition. The Medracar men did their work well; he seems to be unharmed." The man, catching sight of Michael lifting his head, smiled and interrupted something a faint voice from the screen was saying. "Just a moment. He is awake now, sir. He will be ready as soon as you can come over."

The screen went blank, and the plump man turned around. Edging his way toward a sitting position, Michael noticed, suddenly, that he had been dressed in a plain blue robe a little too big for him. But he kept his eyes on the man, who moved toward him, keeping the same elastic smile on his face. "I suppose the first question you want to ask is where you are," the man said. "I suppose you are wondering that."

"I was told not to ask any questions," Michael said. He reached a sitting position and pressed his hands on the couch to steady himself. "And I already know—at least I think I know—that I am in Tandra." He glanced at the buildings beyond the windows. "The commander at the auction complex told me that much."

"Before he drugged you," the man assumed.

"He didn't drug me," Michael said, pinching back grogginess. "I tranquilized myself. I didn't know the tranquilizer was so strong."

"Everything Medron makes is strong," the man said, almost absently. He took a chair and swiveled it to face Michael.

"I know I shouldn't ask questions—" Michael began.

"I don't know where you got that notion," the man said, grinning again, "but there is no limitation on questions while you are in this office. I'll answer you anything I am allowed to."

Michael let himself smile. "I woke before you saw, and heard you talking. You said you hadn't heard from Medracar. So you don't know what happened to the people in the transport room?"

"Transport room?" The man looked blank.

"There was a commander of some kind that kept me from being captured by the Syntac men. He ought to be commended. If he survived, that is. I have a feeling he didn't. Have you had any news at all?"

"No," the man said, then added cheerfully, "but Medracar is in such an uproar that I really haven't tried to get through. I don't know what happened to your commander. But it doesn't matter, does it? The drug has made you dwell on what happened a bit too much, I think. At any rate, you can rest assured that Transvax will suffer no real financial loss from the measures we took to get you out. As I was telling the Director, the remuneration we will receive out of the Tribunal suit should cover all losses—"

Michael touched the cloth on his shoulder. "Would you mind," he asked, "if I stood up and stretched my legs? I'm a little stiff."

"Go right ahead," the man said. "You're a part of the corporation now, so you belong here as much as I do."

Rising to his feet, Michael walked to the windows; his new robes felt heavy and hot in spite of the air-conditioning ducts that put a layer of cool air between him and the glass. He seemed to be on about the twelfth floor of a building. Around him, taller buildings marched away in rows and ranks of glass-cased geometrical shapes. To his left he saw a cluster of tall buildings that he knew must be the seat of the city government. Smoke obscured lower structures leading into the distance on his right, but he fancied he saw the beginning of resource and training suburbs and perhaps the peak of an auction complex thrusting up from the yellow haze. "How big is Tandra?" he asked when he found the plump man's face reflected in the glass.

The man shifted in his seat. "Including all of our resource suburbs, about two-hundred million. Not phenomenal. But adequate. We are an important city because we are very near the world Tribunal in Helcar. This city is about to become important in itself, too, for reasons you will soon discover. But is that the kind of question you really want to ask?"

"No," Michael said, looking at the reflection of the sun on the buildings. "But I'm . . . afraid to ask anything more."

"Afraid?" the man said. "I don't see why? Your future, I think I can assure you, will outstrip your wildest expectations."

Pressing his lips, Michael suppressed a twinge of anticipation. "All right," he said, starting back toward the couch, "if you want my questions, I'll ask them. First of all, I would like to know where I am."

"You're in Tandra. That's old ground."

"But where in Tandra? What office is this?"

"Developmental Affairs, if you want the technical name. We are the part of Transvax that oversees relations between the subcorporations. This entire building is ours, and it is full of offices like this one, most of them smaller; and other men who do as little work as I do." The man punched a button carelessly. "We are administrators here at Developmental Affairs, under only the Secretariat itself in the hierarchy of Transvax. We are the eyes of Transvax for the most part, though occasionally we get our fingers into between-Conglomerate action. We were put in charge of your case, in fact, because the Secretariat itself in Helcar had its hands full with Syntac and the Government. You will be out of our jurisdiction, though, very soon."

"Into whose?"

"If you are wondering who I am," the man went on, seeming not to hear Michael's question, "I am the Assistant

Secretary of Developmental Affairs here in Tandra and was quite happy to take custody of you when your transport arrived in our tube-vaults downstairs, once the Conglomerate Police had secured the area. The Director, the man with whom I was speaking when you woke, wanted to assume responsibility for you immediately when you arrived a few hours ago. But we had to process you, and he was called downstairs by a rumor of a Syntac attack on the Flats. He seems quite impatient to take you."

"The Director?" Michael said, putting his hand to his stomach. "Do you mean the Director of Developmental Affairs?"

"No, no," the Assistant Secretary said; for the first time he seemed irritated. But before he could go on, a sharp buzz interrupted him. He turned his chair away, pressed a pair of buttons, then turned back to Michael. "He's here now," he said. "From the Transvax Space Operations Corporation."

The words thudded in Michael's mind. Up until that moment, possibly because of a lingering effect of the tranquilizer, he had been calm. But mention of the Space Operations Corporation stripped his poise away. From his study of Conglomerate law and affairs, he knew that Space Operations, the fastest growing corporation of the Transvax Conglomerate, was headed by a former advocate, who was now a candidate for the Secretariat itself, and whose power and influence, he had heard, was as great as that of any man on the planet.

He stiffened when the door slid back. For as the man beyond entered, Michael knew he must be the Director himself.

The man was so tall he had to bow his head to move into the office. His unbelted turquoise robe fell from broad shoulders and made him seem a giant, but from his hands and face Michael could tell that he was lean and straight-limbed. His hair and complexion were both dark, and his closely trimmed mustache contrasted with his straight white teeth. His eyes were blue-green like his robe, and they shone so fiercely they seemed to draw all attention toward them. The man wore no device of his office except silver braids, like death-coils, on his shoulders and a silver armband marked with a blue star.

He nodded toward the plump man. "Good morning, Mr. Assistant Secretary," he said. "And good morning, Michael 2112439-851. It's a pleasure to see you whole and well." His bright eyes sized Michael, and Michael, unable to return his gaze, felt as if he were being photographed by an x-ray-equipped computer.

"It's a pleasure to see you, Mr. Director," the Assistant Secretary said. His voice, in comparison to the Director's, sounded nasal. "Your asset seems quite ready to assume your protection."

"Indeed," the Director said, "he seems unharmed. And at least so far, he seems to be everything we bargained for. Do you think he shows promise?"

"Promise for what, sir?"

The Director was still studying Michael. "Never mind. Now, Mr. Assistant Secretary, you will excuse me if I do not stay longer. Urgent matters, this boy not the least of them, call me back to the Flats. Will you kindly check security for my shuttle route. I want no slip-ups now."

Scurrying to his desk, the Assistant Secretary peered into a tiny screen. "All ground areas between here and the Flats are secure," he said.

"Fine," the Director said. "Come with me, Michael."

The Director clamped a heavy hand on his shoulder, and as soon as the Assistant Secretary had opened the office door, the Director guided Michael out into a long, wall-lit corridor that led deeper into the building. Saying nothing, he hurried Michael along, his hand fixed and still on Michael's shoulder until he had to glance at it to convince himself it was not a clamp. The silence of the Director's footfall, the grimness of his expression, and the odd metallic smell of his robe disconcerted Michael so much that by the time they reached the far end of the corridor, he was trembling.

The corridor ended in a glassed-in bay projecting from the building, furnished as a lounge. A medium-sized air-shuttle loomed in most of the window space. It rose and fell slightly as if being swayed by the wind, and the sun sparkled on blue stripes running from its cockpit to its tail. Near the spot where an enclosed boarding ramp connected the ship with the bay, Michael saw a blue star and beneath it in black letters, SPACE OPERATIONS CORPORATION.

After they passed over the ramp into the air-shuttle itself, Michael found that it was not furnished with the rows of seats to which he was accustomed. Instead the entire interior of the ship except the cockpit was open. Broad skylights gaped overhead, and the carpeted walls were hung with decorative panels and narrow mirrors. A few thickly padded chairs were scattered around the cabin, but most were clumped around panorama portholes, from which sunlight poured in to stripe the blue carpet with gold. Michael wanted to ask what such an airship was used for, but a glance at the Director made him seal his lips.

The Director steered Michael to the nearest clump of chairs, where both of them sat down. The Director signaled the pilot through an intercom, and the boarding passage retracted. Soon the Developmental Affairs building drifted away, and Michael peered out of the window as the complexes of glass dropped silently away below them.

"Would you like something to eat?" the Director asked presently. And when Michael shook his head, "To drink?"

"No," Michael said, though he was thirsty.

"Make yourself comfortable," the Director said. "This will not be a short ride."

Reclining a little, Michael tried to smile. But he found it hard to relax in the Director's presence, particularly since the Director's eyes, whenever he dared glance at them, rested on him. He wished he had had more of a chance to question the Assistant Secretary, for he had the feeling the Director was one of the people the commander at the auction complex had meant when he said not to ask questions. Dozens of inquiries were rising in him, both old ones and new ones. Yet he swallowed them and occupied himself looking out the window, pretending to be absorbed with the faint patterns of the city below.

He was being taken to a place called the Flats; that much he had gleaned. But just what this place was and what he would do there, he could not guess. He suspected that he might finish his training as a special advocate for the Space Operations Corporation. Still, reflecting on what had happened at the auction complex in Medracar, he decided it might be something more. He could not forget what the Assistant Secretary had said about his future.

Abruptly the Director spoke. "Michael," he said, "have you ever considered space? Have you ever thought what might be out there, beyond the boundaries of our world?"

"When I was a child in the resource suburb," Michael said, "I often looked at the stars. And I have studied a little astronomy."

The Director seemed to swallow this with contempt. "Let me put it this way," he said, smoothing his mustache with a flick of his finger. "What have you heard about what Transvax plans for space exploration?"

"I have heard nothing," Michael said. He added quickly, reading the Director's stare. "It is my understanding that the Space Operations Corporation hasn't yet officially released its plans."

"Quite correct," the Director said, his face bland again. "But if you were to guess what those plans might be?"

"If I were to guess, I would only be mistaken," Michael said, peering out the window again. "As I said, my background—"

"Your background is adequate," the Director said. "Guess."

"I expect the first step would be to achieve Vaxan orbit."

"Quite right. But that step has already been taken. All

three of the Conglomerates have orbiting satellites. Transvax has an orbiting laboratory. What do you see as the next step?"

Michael felt sure he was being quizzed. "I imagine the next step would be to land a spacecraft on the moon or on the nearest planets of our solar system, Phoros and Anakra."

"You are quite sure this would be the next step?"

"I think it would be," Michael answered. "It seems only logical."

"Indeed." the Director said, leaning back in his chair, "logical. What you have just described is what I expected you to describe; if you had said anything else, I would lose faith in our master computer's selective ability. Syntac and Medron, indeed, even half of the assets of Transvax, expect the same thing. They assume that our space probes will planet-hop through this solar system, beginning, as you say, with our moon and our nearest planetary neighbors. But that is what we want them to believe. We want none of them to guess," the Director stared at Michael, "that they are all dead wrong."

"Wrong?" Michael said. "How?"

"Think about it," the Director said. "What could Transvax do if it reached the moon?"

"Set up a scientific research base," Michael ventured. "Or maybe establish some kind of industry to tap the moon's mineral resources."

"Any large-scale transport of moon-mined minerals would be too expensive," the Director countered. "As for science, may it go to the dogs! Science, Michael, is useful only in so far as it provides financial return—or paves the way for financial return. We are in a business, in competition with our Conglomerate counterparts. We cannot afford to waste our resources trying to manage that bleak chip of rock out there. We will not send a spacecraft to our moon."

"Phoros then. Or Anakra."

"Phoros," the Director replied, "is so close to the sun

that its day side is molten and its night side frozen. It has little or no atmosphere. What would Transvax want with a world like that? And Anakra, even though it has an atmosphere, is a frigid desert. A probe we sent out five years ago has sent back photographs of volcanic eruptions and shifts in the Anakran crust. It, too, is a world not worth exploiting."

"Then I can't fathom what other plans you might have," Michael said. He felt as if he had missed an obvious answer. "Surely if Anakra is useless to you, the five Outer Planets will be, too. And certainly the technology for interstellar travel is years away."

"Decades. Centuries, perhaps, if at all."

"Then for the present," Michael said, lowering his eyebrows, "space must hold nothing profitable for you to explore."

A slow smile crept across the Director's lips, a smile that Michael found almost as alarming as his grimness. "You have answered my questions well, and now that I have whetted your curiosity, I will begin to explain why you are here—why we paid two thousand chronas for you, and why Syntac would pay twice that amount to have you dead."

Michael took in a sharp breath. "Tell me," he said, the flesh of his arms suddenly cold, "please."

Rising to his feet, the Director motioned for Michael to rise. He brought him to the center of the room, then took a palm-sized device from his robes and pointed at a screen set among the skylights. Immediately bright stars appeared on a black background; they seemed to be moving away from each other, just perceptibly, as if the camera were being moved toward them. "A simulation we use," the Director said, and he pressed another button on his device. The stars melted away to a many-ringed diagram that Michael soon recognized as a representation of the solar system. "The innermost ring is the orbit of Phoros. The blue dot on the third ring is Anakra."

"And the silver dot on the second," Michael assumed,

"is our world, Vax." He stopped himself. "But there are two spots on the second orbit."

"There are indeed," the Director said. He worked a pair of buttons on his device. The dots on the chart began to revolve slowly, the two on the second ring, one silver and one black, remaining opposite of one another.

Michael looked at the Director suddenly, his lips parting in understanding. "You mean," he said in a low voice, "that there is a fourth world among the Inner Planets, a world that orbits on the same path as our own earth?"

"To simplify it, yes. This world, as you see here, constantly remains opposite ours, so it has never been visible in our sky. It has never been named or known on our world —until only a few years ago. And even now, no one on Vax has ever actually seen it."

Michael stared at the chart. "Then how do we know it exists?"

"Our first clue came a decade ago, when one of our scientists was researching gravitational pulls among the planets and the sun. Each planet leaves a 'print' in the sun's shape according to its gravitational pull, just as the moon prints its gravity on the earth with tides. This astronomer matched all the prints on the sun with known planets. But one print, a print with the dimensions of our own world, remained. Its only explanation could be another planet, one orbiting on the far side of the sun from us."

"That seems to be slim evidence," Michael said.

"Slim enough that the other Conglomerates, with the less sophisticated equipment we installed in their satellites, as yet have no notion it exists," the Director said, moving to a seat again. "In the last ten years, we have targeted our resources on proving our scientist's notion. We have found an unexplained sparkle on our probes' radio messages from space. A mysterious trail of oxygen molecules in our orbit too dense for only one world to make—"

"Are you suggesting, then, that this other world, this counter-Vax, is similar to this planet?" He glanced at the window. "Are you saying that there is another Vax on the far side of the sun?"

"No," the Director said, moving to his seat again, "not 'another Vax,' though we theorize that in mass and climate it is quite parallel. Instead, Michael, this world is somewhat a mirror of Vax. That, I suppose, is why one of our more romantic scientists named it Mirrorvax."

"Mirrorvax," Michael repeated, with a sudden and unexplained chill that made him remember gazing at the stars as a child.

"Mirrorvax, then." the Director went on, "becomes the target of Transvax's first reach into space. As you can see from the chart, it is not an easy planet to reach; because it orbits opposite us, it is much more distant than either Phoros or Anakra. And guiding a ship there will be much more difficult, because we are blind to Mirrorvax. And there is the added risk of losing the ship once it has gone behind the sun, because any communication will be garbled by the intense solar radiation through which it will have to pass."

"But wouldn't it be simpler to place a ship out of Vaxan gravity, so it would arrive at Mirrorvax simply by being stationary in orbit?" Michael asked. "Or send the ship on the orbit around the sun, so that it would meet Mirrorvax in a few months?"

"Good observation," the Director said. "It would be simpler to do what you suggest. If space were empty. But along with the two planets on this orbit is a light asteroid belt. Most of the asteroids are scarcely bigger than dust particles, but a few are the size of mountains. We dare not let a ship chance encountering one of them. Thus our ship must cut the Vaxan orbit by making a tighter arc around the sun. There are other, theoretical ways. But this route, our scientists are sure, is the most likely to bring us success. And we must have success. A try for Mirrorvax will be dangerous, costly, and difficult, so much so that initial failure will doom any further attempt."

"Then why go to Mirrorvax at all?"

The Director leaned forward, his eyes glittering. "For three good reasons and possibly more. To begin with, scientific exploration of Mirrorvax is liable to be extremely profitable, because Mirrorvax is similar enough to our own world that it might provide useful parallels—"

"Life, you mean?" Michael asked.

"We don't know whether life exists on Mirrorvax. If it does, we cannot guess what forms it takes. Thus the exploration. And thus the second reason. If life does exist on Mirrorvax, and if that life is in any way similar to ours, there is a good chance we may find Mirrorvax habitable, unlike Phoros or Anakra."

"Colonization?" Michael said, increasingly interested. "I begin to see the possibilities. A whole new world for Vaxans to tame—"

"For Transvax to tame," the Director said, suppressing a smile. "For Transvax to use and profit from. Mirrorvax," he said, gripping the arms of his chair, "is the key to making Transvax supreme among the Conglomerates, once and for all. The other corporations, as I said, have been kept blind to Mirrorvax so far—we build their satellites, and we have made sure our secret is secure. For you see, Michael, the glorious third reason for going to Mirrorvax, and going soon, is that we—a few of us in the Space Operations Corporation and of course the members of the Secretariat—are the only ones who even know Mirrorvax exists."

"I know, now that you have told me," Michael said. "Why did you share your secret?"

"You are shrewd indeed," the Director said with an approving nod. "I think you understand already that Transvax has invested so much in you because it wishes to use you in the most critical of positions."

"I understand the expense and trouble Transvax has absorbed to bring me here," Michael said solemnly. "And by Vax, I will do all I can to be worth what Transvax has spent. But I still don't understand, sir, how I fit into all of this."

"Ah," the Director said, glancing out the window. "We seem to be descending. You might fasten your safety straps, Michael, because docking here is sometimes rough, the way the wind streams across these Flats."

Catching sight of a broad, empty horizon rising toward him, Michael put his arms through the two loops affixed to the back of his chair. The Director, however, made no attempt to do the same; he only gripped the arms of his chair with heavily veined hands and craned his neck toward the window. Michael followed his eyes toward the earth and saw for the first time objects in the haze—featureless buildings spread in sprawling complexes on the right. On his left, something like a long silver finger glinted, something cylindrical and massive that swung out of view as the air-shuttle curved sunward toward a landing pad among the largest of the buildings.

The Director's eyes lifted to Michael's. "What you have just seen." he said in a voice as crisp as the one he had used with the Assistant Secretary, "is the product of five years' work and almost a quarter of Transvax's total financial output. What you glimpsed," he went on as the faces of concrete buildings loomed up in the portholes, "is the instrument of Transvax's future, and the vehicle of your own. You have seen the ship that will in a quarter of a chrona be lifted up and pointed toward invisible Mirrorvax. You have seen *The Arm of Transvax*, the greatest achievement of Transvax since its beginning; possibly the greatest in all of mankind's history. You, Michael, have seen destiny."

Michael's throat went dry. He was numbed by a realization that made him fumble off his straps and pitch as if sickened when he stood up. The Director smiled when he saw the color of Michael's face, and gripping Michael's arm, he said. "Yes, Michael. In ninety days, when *The Arm of Transvax* reaches for Mirrorvax, you will be aboard her."

THE CRADLE
OF THE DARK

IN THE FIRST tiled passageway, the Director's boots echoed, and Michael's barefoot strides seemed to make no sound at all. He swayed as he walked, for his legs threatened to give way beneath him. At last he managed to speak. "I need an explanation," he said.

The Director glanced back at him. "Of what?"

"Of why I am to journey on *The Arm of Transvax*," Michael said.

"You are to journey on *The Arm of Transvax*," the Director said, picking up his pace again, "because you are the property of the Space Operations Corporation, and that is what we wish you to do. You will be the third of three astronauts we are preparing to send to Mirrorvax. Do you need to know more?"

"No," Michael said, with effort, remembering his debt to Transvax. "But I would like to know why you chose me to send. After all, I have had none of the training I'm sure is necessary—"

They rounded a corner into another passage. "You will be trained."

"But ninety days is so short a time," Michael objected. "You don't mean to tell me that, having planned this operation for at least five years, you left the training of your astronauts until now."

"You're right," the Director said. "We haven't. You are a replacement."

Michael began jogging to keep up. "A replacement?"

"One of our original astronauts was killed a few days ago," the Director said, keeping his eyes ahead. "He died in an air-shuttle crash between here and Tandra. We think that Medron was responsible, but we can't prove it. At any rate, we are one short. That is where you come in."

"But you must have trained back-up astronauts."

"We did. Several. But our security was too lax. Several of the astronauts died of some kind of poisoning—Medron's work again. The rest went down with the same shuttle that killed our third man."

Michael folded his arms. "It sounds as if being an astronaut is a risky business, even while still on Vax."

"We have stepped up our security now, if that is what you mean," the Director said with a sour smile. "None of you will leave this compound until the spaceflight. The constant low clouds here keep the Flats from Syntac or Medron surveillance, but they seem to know our operation is somewhere in this area. That's why they have tried to destroy every shuttle sent from here to Tandra; that's why our trainees died in a crash and of poisoning on a visit to the city; that's why Syntac broke every rule in the Statutes trying to kill you when our computer began bidding so high for you. Neither Syntac nor Medron knows about Mirrorvax or our project, but they know we are up to something big, and they are doing all they can to stop us. But they won't. We are too far along now. Here. This is the door we want."

They moved through an opening into a high-roofed room that reminded Michael of a gymnasium; other doors opened from it on all sides, and a panel wall on the far end slid back at the touch of the Director's hand device. It revealed a large computer room where blue-robed men and women were working. All of them stood up and faced the Director, who brushed past them to reach another door and beyond that a conference room with a table and chairs like those aboard the shuttle.

"Sit down." he told Michael as soon as the door had closed behind them. He activated a wall intercom, snapped something about sending someone down, then lowered himself into a chair at the end of the table. Michael, a little breathless, propped his elbows on the table and put his cheeks in his hands. "Sir," he said when he saw the Director glaring at him, "I still don't understand why you chose me. Wouldn't it have been much easier for you to train one of your own people—someone in your own cor poration?"

"If you must know," the Director said, "if you must have answers to all your questions now, you were our most logical choice. Unless you have grown since your last measurements recorded in the Vaxan resource computer, you are just the same size as our former astronaut. This is important because you must be able to wear the considerable amount of pre-fitted gear—spacesuits, for instance—that we prepared for the first man. Your weight must balance in the ship as his would have. But size was only one of our considerations."

"Since we had no trained replacement," the Director went on, linking his hands over his knee, "we wanted someone who would be relatively easy to train; that is, someone who had had training in the basics already. Vaxan law, as the Government teaches it, is excellent general background; it would be such even if I were not biased in favor of law-trainees, having been an advocate myself. We wanted, in addition, someone not too old and not too young, someone with no previous loyalties to other Conglomerates, and someone, like yourself, with no alternative but us and our programs—these were necessary qualities. Since the Government has so few half-trained advocates, you were not hard to choose. When we found that you matched up to our needs, we simply requested that your training suburb put you up for auction. We paid two thousand chronas for you, a few dozen lives, and you were ours. It was that simple."

"Now comes the hard part, for me at least." Michael said. "Now I have to make myself worth what you paid for me."

"Precisely." The Director narrowed his eyes. "It is absolutely essential that you do so."

For the first time Michael began breathing more easily. He laid his hands on the table and looked at them. The future, as the Assistant Secretary had said it would be, seemed incredible. A few days before he had been Government stock, with a dim and narrow outlook. Then for a few hours he had felt the sting of being recyclage. How the word prickled in his spine, even now. But Transvax had made him worth more. They had made him worth at least two thousand chronas and the attention of Assistant Secretaries and Directors. They had reinforced the notion he had always had that he was something better than Government stock or recyclage. And he would prove to them— and himself—that he was.

A moment later the door to the control room opened again, and a man and a woman came in. They dipped their heads to the Director, then stood at attention, hands behind their backs, throats stiff with their chins upraised; but their eyes, the woman's ice-colored ones and the man's earth-orange ones, wandered to Michael and remained there. Both of them wore white uniforms with legs ending in knee-high boots. The woman's straight black hair hid most of her cheeks, and the tart curl of her lips reminded Michael of a photograph he had seen of an ancient Vaxan princess: the features of her face seemed dark and chiseled, as if she were a representative of a cruel imperial race. The man's face, however, was smooth as sanded wood, and the slight frown he wore made him seem pensive rather than stern.

Seeming to note mutual reactions with some amusement, the Director stood up. "These, Michael," he said, "are your future companions on *The Arm of Transvax*. This is Judy, our scientific specialist—she began working on this project long before she was chosen to be an astronaut. And the sullen one is Jeremy; he is our technician."

The man smiled at him, but the woman narrowed her eyes. "And is this boy to be Mark's replacement? Where did you find him? Is he trained?"

"Yes; none of your business; and no," the Director answered, glowering at her. "This is Michael. You will accept him as you did Mark and do all you can to accelerate his training. Is that understood?"

Jeremy nodded, but Judy, closing her lips, let her hair fall over her eyes. "Is that understood?" the Director repeated.

Her face snapped up to his. Her hair fell away to expose a sneer. "Yes," she said. With a disdainful glance at Michael, she nodded to the Director, whirled, and left the room. The Director sighed, put a finger to his mustache, then said to Jeremy, "Show him to his cubicle. Then take him to meet Gregor and Alan and the other instructors. He must begin training this afternoon."

Jeremy brought Michael to a pair of connected rooms on a corridor leading away from the gymnasium. The furnishings he saw reminded him of his room at the advocate training suburb, except there were more of them. And one wall of the deeper room was devoted to a closet where a dozen white uniforms and a few peculiar-looking silver suits hung. Jeremy took one of the uniforms down and handed it to Michael. Michael held it up but made no move to put it on, for on a square of cloth above the pocket, between blue stars, was printed MARK 4495496–002. He looked to Jeremy, who only scratched at his own name tag and averted his eyes. Sighing, Michael shed his robe and put the suit on. Jeremy helped him with the fastenings on the back and with the boots, which seemed a tight fit.

Michael was still straightening the shoulders of the uniform when he followed Jeremy from the room. For no matter what the Director had said, the uniform was a little too big.

That afternoon Gregor, a wizened-looking man with a catlike gray mustache, had his assistants set up foam manikins against the empty wall of the gymnasium. He then took a fistful of silver cords from a box, passing them first to Jeremy and then to Judy. Determined to be forceful, Michael reached out for them when Gregor moved up to him.

The trainer drew the cords back out of his reach. "Your gloves, man," he said in a rusty-sounding voice. "Good Vax, where are your gloves?"

"Gloves?" Michael said, suddenly horrified.

"You haven't thrown a death-cord before, then?" Gregor assumed.

"No, not ever. Should I have brought gloves?"

Flexing her fingers in her own gloves, Judy turned to Michael. "Check your waist pocket," she said. "That's where gloves are kept: I never knew Mark to be without a pair in his uniform."

After a moment of digging, Michael drew out a pair of thin-skinned gloves, which he pulled on clumsily. Gregor then handed him a pair of coils. "Rule one with death-coils is never to touch them without proper gloves. These aren't activated generally, but now and again you come across one that's live, and if you so much as graze it with your thumb, you can kiss coil-throwing good-bye forever. You bring a coil to life by taking both ends of it—like this." He demonstrated for Michael, who did his best to imitate. "Then you pull sharply—like that. If the coil snaps as mine did, it is activated and ready to throw."

Michael stared down at the steel cord in his gloves, and fancied he heard it humming faintly. He remembered how the cords had twined around the Syntac men in the auction chamber. "Now, all you have to do is throw it; you'll get the knack of it with practice." Gregor added, "After I'm out of the way, of course."

Michael let go of one end of the coil, swung it behind him, then hurled it forward with all his might. The thing whistled toward its target, but it skimmed over the manikin's shoulder and fell harmlessly against the far wall. Judy's cord, released only a moment later, cracked like a whip around a manikin's neck, toppling it to the ground.

"The art takes practice," Gregor said, eyeing Judy's work.

When Jeremy's throw brought down a second manikin, Michael asked, "Will we learn to use barb-throwers?"

At this Judy laughed, showing her teeth. "We would be violating the Statutes if we did. Barb-throwers are Syntac's domain, just as food synthesis, clothing synthesis, and housing are their market. We could no more use barb-throwers than we could use Medron's venom-eggs or try to muscle into Medron's jurisdiction by selling medical supplies or computers. According to the Statutes, Transvax handles transportation and communications and death-coils. Nothing more."

"I'm afraid Judy is taking advantage of your innocence," Gregor said. "Barb-throwers and venom-eggs are illegal for us to use, but you will learn mastery of them all. On Mirrorvax you will need to be able to defend yourselves."

Michael glared at Judy, then snapped his second coil to life. On his next throw he made the farthest manikin crumple to the floor.

"I trust you have had time to memorize the regulation package I gave you," the instructor Alan said to Michael when they took seats on opposite sides of the council table. "All of the material I gave you is vital."

"I understand," Michael said. "I've been here for four days now, and I've had a little time to study in the evenings when I'm finished with weapon practice and simulation training."

"Good. Are you ready to answer some questions about what you read?"

"Yes," Michael said, "I am."

The instructor leaned forward. "To begin with, then, tell me the first objective of your mission to Mirrorvax."

"To gather all possible information about the world called Mirrorvax: about whatever is around, near, or on it."

"Which means, so far as your part in it?"

"That I will assist Judy in her scientific investigations on our approach to the planet and for six Vaxan days after our landing or for as long as she requires assistance with her astronomical, meteorological, and biological measurements. I am also to assist Jeremy in any repairs necessary on the AOT upon landing and in any pursuits he as commander feels are needed upon our arrival there. I am also to make and record my own observations and questions on tape and in script and am required to voice any fears, concerns, or insights to both Jeremy and Judy."

"You memorize very well, Michael."

Michael let himself smile slightly. He thanked himself for missing a little sleep to study the regulations packet. "I studied law before this," he said. "Most of our curriculum required memorization."

"I see that the Director, as usual, knew what he was doing when he arranged for you. Now tell me your mission's second objective."

Michael glanced at the ceiling. "Once the base camp has been established and once Jeremy and Judy no longer require my assistance, I will take leave of the ship to follow a path prescribed by an agreement between the three of us, returning at a prescribed time if it is within my power. I am again to make verbal and written record of anything I see, hear, encounter, or sense that may be of any importance to Transvax researchers. I will document my route with photographs, take no unnecessary risks, and under no circumstances venture farther than my supplies of food and oxygen take me."

46

"And if you encounter a life form?""

Michael shrugged. "That depends, doesn't it?"

The instructor nodded. "On what does it depend?"

Michael took a deep breath. "Minute forms of life I cannot see, so I am required to, at intervals, take samples of Mirrorvaxan soil, where my knowledge of astrobiology suggests such life may thrive. If I come upon a life form small enough to be carried on my person, I will place it in an appropriate pouch, carefully noting the place of its origin on my map."

"You have memorized even the fine print, haven't you?"

"If the life form is too large to carry with me, I am to photograph it and document it as best as I can, noting such things as its dimensions, if plantlike; and its form of locomotion, if animal-like. I am to—"

"What if the life form is hostile?" the instructor interrupted. "What will you do then?"

Michael felt his temples go tight. "That possibility was not listed in the material you gave me."

"No, it wasn't," the instructor said, grinning. "But though you will be given directives on this particular situation later on, I'd like to see how well you think on your feet. Our materials after all cannot conceivably prepare you for all you will contact on Mirrorvax."

"How do you mean 'hostile'?" Michael asked, stalling for time.

"Suppose, for instance, you are coming around a boulder and find yourself face to face with a fanged creature about the size of a man that begins following you after you back away from it?"

"Is it running after me or walking?" Michael asked.

"Does it matter?"

"Yes." Michael said. "Because if it is walking, it might be intelligent and not really hostile, and I might eventually come to communicate with it. But if it is running—with the intention of hurting me—I might do something more drastic."

47

"I'm afraid your thinking needs a little correction there," the instructor said. "I told you the thing had fangs. It could be dangerous even if it is intelligent—especially if it is intelligent—even if it walks—or slithers slowly, as may happen. Danger is danger, Michael, and on a mission as important as this one, you can't take any chances. Not any. Do you understand what I'm saying? This is one case where you kill first and ask questions later. Get that straight. *Take no unnecessary risks.* That is what it says in the material, isn't it?"

Michael wanted to object that the material did not say to use his death-cord before his mind, but he only nodded. "Why do you think," the instructor went on, "that we have taken such pains to arm you with every weapon known to us? Why do you think you saw that hold full of artillery on the plans of the AOT you saw yesterday? Good Vax, Michael, we're not sending you across the solar system just to have you butchered."

Shivering, Michael nodded again.

"Next question. What is your third and last objective?"

This one Michael knew best. "We are to complete all our surveys and investigations by the end of sixty Vaxan days, even if our oxygen and food supplies provide us more flexibility. Under no circumstances are we to delay beyond that time, even if a crew member is missing—"

"Do you know why that is?" the instructor broke in.

"No."

"That clause was added by a member of the Transvax Secretariat itself because the Space Operations Corporation and the other factions of the Conglomerate that support us are under tremendous pressure to make this project a fast, clean success. The cost of the project is after all phenomenal, and if there is a slip-up of any kind, if the AOT does not return, the Space Operations Corporation will most likely be cut back or even disbanded. There will be no second attempt. To narrow down the possibilities for disaster, so to speak, a time limit of sixty days was set, to give the crew enough time for their observations, but to guard against too long a stay. Every day you spend in that alien environment only compounds the chances that something bad will happen. I can see that that makes sense to you. Good. Now go ahead with what you were saying."

"Uh . . . under no circumstances . . . even if a crew member is missing. We are to triple-check navigational and technical preparations for the home journey. We are to make sure all our samples and observation records are properly placed and secure, including any samples of life, living or dead, with which we have made appropriate relations—"

"*Appropriate relations,*" the instructor echoed. "Which means—?"

"Everything we bring back will be dead," Michael said dully.

"Very good. But don't tell our scientists those were our instructions."

Michael glared across the table. He repeated, "Including any samples of life, *dead,* with which we have made appropriate relations."

"You learn fast," the instructor said, swiveling his chair away. "I will tell the Director"—he licked his lips—"that you are progressing satisfactorily."

"This," Gregor said when he had given each of the three a small silver box affixed to a chain with a flat rectangle attached, "is one of the most recent and useful breakthroughs from our Corporation scientists, and if life indeed exists on Mirrorvax—intelligent life, that is—you will find it indispensable. For the present, however," he added, cocking an eyebrow, "you will find it confusing and frustrating."

"What is it?" Judy asked. "A blank identification tag?"

"It is a translator," Gregor said, pacing toward the head of the council room table. You put it over your head as if it were a neck chain and center the flat rectangle on your collar bone. Then reach to the back of the chain, where

49

you will find a microphone box that is connected to the rectangle by an almost invisible but durable thread. Press the box against the skin just inside your ear. It should stick." Michael, following Gregor's instruction, put the chain over his head, found the box and touched it to his ear as Gregor had instructed. At first the connecting thread tickled his neck, and a mosquito-like buzzing in his ear made him want to tear the thread away, but he held back his irritation long enough to realize that everything Gregor was saying was being repeated, a split second later, by the nodule in his ear. The echo-effect was annoying and even dizzying, and watching the others, he saw that their reactions were the same.

"Odd, isn't it?" Gregor said with a half-smile.

Michael said yes aloud, to hear how his own voice would sound over the translator. "You may need all sixty-two days before the flight to get used to it. But now let me demonstrate how it works." Gregor opened an odd-looking book on the table. "I'm about to read you a passage in one of the old Vaxan languages that no one has bothered with since the advent of Universal Speech." Gregor began reading odd, overextended syllables, but though Michael by no means understood them, the voice in his ear echoed the foreign words with familiar ones. By concentrating on the nodule, Michael was able to follow what seemed to be a dialogue between two people with odd names.

"Great Transvax!" Judy said when Gregor broke off. "This is amazing. How does it work?"

"If I understood the processes," Gregor said, "I would be in the lab inventing things, not here answering your questions. But it has something to do with brain wave modulation, because it was necessary for me to learn enough of this language to know what I was saying. Apparently the device cannot function otherwise. If I were to give you a nonsense word, the device would not translate it, no matter what I was thinking—the translator seems to work on the basis of both the mental and vocal."

"It will translate Old Vaxan," Judy said. "But will it

translate a language alien to its designers, such as we may hear on Mirrorvax?"

"The device, I am told, is far from perfected and quite unpredictable. But the scientists who developed it assure me that it should provide at least sketchy translation for any vocalized language—"

"What if Mirrorvaxans use sign language or another non-vocal form?" Judy asked.

"Then," Gregor said, "you will be quite on your own."

"And what if we want to speak their language back to them?" Michael added.

"You will have to pick up whatever you can through listening to them and to your translator. But I ought to point out that you will most likely not need this device at all. Even if a language-speaking species lives on Mirrorvax, your near-at-hand conversations, considering the instructions we have given you, are likely to be rather one-sided."

Michael had had nightmares the first few nights he spent in his new rooms. He had at first dreamed of Mark, the dead astronaut he had replaced. Later he dreamed of Judy, who was almost always sneering at him; and Jeremy, who in dreams said little more than in waking. But since Michael had always been taught to think of dreams as primitive manifestations of his mind, and because his nightmares faded away when the days of rigorous training began to exhaust him, he thought little about them. But just before the halfway mark in his training, the nightmares returned.

Some of them were about Judy and Jeremy, as the first ones had been; for even after working long hours and weeks with them, he felt he understood them little more than when he had first met them. Judy continued to scorn and avoid him. Jeremy, though he seemed amiable enough, said very little; if he spoke at all, he did so haltingly and in a hoarse whisper, and his conversation was clipped and awkward. To make matters worse, Michael had no free time with them, in part because of his intense schedule of

51

training, and in part because all three of them were quar
tered in different parts of the complex for reasons of security. And so they appeared to him while he slept as
phantoms, in new and dreadful shapes.

But more disconcerting still was another nightmare. He
could never remember more than shreds of it after waking:
fleeting glimpses of reeling stars; a sound like mournful
horns, heard from far off; and a smell something like burning but more sweet. He dreaded the dream less than the
waking, for it was lying in the darkness afterward that
troubled him. He felt then as if he were alone, as if all the
complex at the Flats lay empty under the stars, as if Vax
were barren, as if the very universe itself was hollow and
silent. The feeling often became so intense that he closed
his hands over his mouth to keep from crying out. And always when the waking siren came, he felt shame; for he
knew that loneliness was an anachronism, not a word; and
that what he felt, or imagined he felt, was like his dreams—
a vestige of human weakness and savagery that he would
do best to bury or destroy.

When thirty days of training time remained, Alan and
Gregor, now convinced that all three astronauts could use
artillery and death-cords, discontinued weapons practice in
favor of physical training. The heart of the program was to
be running, ten times around the opening in the building
where the shuttles landed. The place was bare, lacking anything of interest but the shuttle pad and the enclosing
buildings. Perhaps it was boredom that made Judy talk to
him on the third day, but maybe it was that Jeremy was
missing; he had seemed more quiet than ever that morning,
and early in the afternoon he had gone to the infirmary.

Michael and Judy paced themselves together on a beaten
track of earth. Michael's stride was longer but Judy's
swifter, and for the first lap it seemed to be a race between
them; but when they passed Gregor, he shouted for them
not to wear themselves out, so Michael slowed obediently,

and Judy sank back to a restless trot.

"Have you run before?" Judy asked him when they had finished half the lap.

"Yes," he said. "When I was a resource. As part of my training."

Something he had said seemed to amuse her; the crook in her lip deepened, and he imagined he heard her laughing, though it might only have been her stressed breathing.

"What about you?" he said in a moment.

She chose not to answer but said instead, after they had passed Gregor again, "Jeremy is not well. But I don't think he is sick."

"I don't see how you can tell, either way, even if you know him better than I do," Michael said. He hesitated but went on, "Since I have been here, I haven't heard him say more than a few dozen words. I am beginning to wonder if the Director is right when he calls him sullen—"

"The Director," Judy snapped, "is a fool. And you are a fool, too, if you fault Jeremy because of what he does or doesn't say." She tossed her hair over her shoulder and began running more swiftly. "Jeremy is not mysterious when you have read his records, as I have. He is brilliant, possibly the brightest technician Transvax has ever produced. But that is not why he became an astronaut. And that is not why he does not speak. He is quiet because he must be: half his vocal chords were surgically removed when he was first bought by Transvax. As a technician in training, he spoke out against a member of the Secretariat who wanted Transvax scientists to develop new weapons. Punishment for rebellion is of course termination, but Transvax could not afford to lose his mind. So they took away part of his voice as a warning. In the three years since, he has seen Transvax with new eyes: that is the way his records put it. Now he—like you and me—is a favored asset of Transvax. But the scar on his throat still shows."

Michael remembered seeing no scar, but he shuddered in spite of himself. They passed Gregor again, and he said,

53

"Transvax showed mercy to Jeremy, it seems. But even so, it is odd that the Director should trust him—"

"The Director does not," Judy retorted. "The Director trusts no one. That is how he became the Director."

"But what about Jeremy? Why would he want to serve Transvax so well? He must have done much to become an astronaut. Why did he do it?"

"Why do any of us do it?" Judy quickened her pace. "We do it because we have no choice. We belong to Transvax. And we are what Transvax needs."

Michael nodded. "I suppose that Jeremy feels as much in debt to them for the mercy they showed him as I do for the price they paid for me in the auction chamber—"

"The auction chamber?" Judy said. "You were auctioned? When?"

"Just before I was brought here, of course."

Tilting her head back, Judy frowned. "I had had the impression you were Transvax stock, but I see I was wrong. Where were you before you were *auctioned?*"

"I was in training," Michael said, feeling warm around the ears, "in training at Medracar to become an advocate."

"An advocate? Then you are Government stock," she said, leering at the realization. Her eyes flashed at him, and the sharpness in them made her look once again like a barbarian princess. "Then you were auctioned a second time," she said, "as *recyclage!*"

He bit his lip and tried to outdistance her, but she kept up with him, eyes glittering, lips curving fiercely. "And the Director thought you could replace Mark, who was six years Transvax stock and four years the Space Corporation's. Oh indeed," she almost bellowed, "indeed the Director is a fool! And you, Michael, are still only recyclage!"

Michael did not see Jeremy again for several days. But when he did, he noted a hair-thin white line on his throat, and found himself both repulsed by Jeremy and fascinated by him; the thought that his man had once opposed Transvax made his lip curl, but Jeremy's constant warm expression baffled him and drew him involuntarily nearer. Now observing Jeremy as if he had not seen him before, Michael decided that the Director's and his own reaction to Jeremy was wrong: Jeremy was not sullen.

He was careful with words but not with smiles; he seemed to smile almost without provocation: when he missed a throw with the cord; when Judy showed frustration with the translating device; or when he looked at Michael. Michael had earlier thought the smiles to be derisive, but he soon began to suspect that most of them were not.

Fifteen days before the flight, the three of them were taken to a launchpad to tour *The Arm of Transvax*, which had been erected between two steel towers. From a distance it looked like a silver finger, and from near at hand a massive cyclindrical skyscraper. During the entire excursion, Michael noted, Jeremy let the others go first and once held an airlock door open while they passed through. And his orange eyes, Michael noticed, missed no detail of whatever they passed.

Upon their return from the launch area, Gregor announced that physical training would be dropped in favor of instruction with a newly constructed set of space simulators. The most important of these was a great metal egg in a gymnasium-like room at the far end of the complex. It was a navigation simulator whose design was precisely like the one in *The Arm of Transvax*. Theoretically it would give Jeremy and Michael some practical experience. Michael was a little nervous the first day he tried it out, and he would have caused a simulated crash shortly after lift-off if Jeremy had not corrected his error. But by the second time they practiced in the simulator, his knowledge of the controls had increased so he could guide the mock AOT through clouds of animated stars to an easy three-point landing on a distant planet that looked remarkably like the chalk hills on the far side of the Flats. And after the third time, using the controls became so automatic that he found even the more ticklish problems boring.

Michael soon discovered that he was not the only one who was bored. After their third simulated voyage, Jeremy began to talk, turning to his instruments only occasionally. Their conversations were awkward in the darkness of the egg under the simulated stars, and at first Michael found Jeremy's rough whisper hard to understand. But gradually both of them came to speak more freely, and though they talked about themselves and each other, Michael found himself looking forward to the hours spent in the egg. Strangely enough, too, his nightmares, once he had mentioned them to Jeremy, began to occur less frequently, until they did not come at all.

"I have had nightmares, often, too," Jeremy said. "The scientists tell you that they are primitive and foreign to us, but they are not. They are parts of us, parts we sometimes don't see in daylight." This did little to comfort Michael, and he thought Transvax might not approve of Jeremy holding such a view. But talking about his dreams had made them seem less frightening.

Once when Michael asked Jeremy to tell about one of his own nightmares, Jeremy remained silent for a long time, then leaned back in his seat and croaked, his eyes fixed on the stars above them:

> "This is the cradle of the dark;
> We lie with bones and watch the stars—
> To fathom how to quench their fire
> So we may sleep in peace."

Chilled by the beat of his words, Michael said little more to Jeremy the rest of that flight and was not much comforted when Jeremy explained that the words had been arranged after an ancient art. For he knew the words had been Jeremy's, and so had the art; and imagining the egg as a cradle, he could understand why Transvax feared Jeremy's voice enough to have taken half of it out.

The incident, however, soon lost itself in the heightening

frenzy of training, and both of them avoided talk of nightmares during the simulator sessions thereafter, which became increasingly rare.

Each morning Gregor, Alan, and scientists from the main research base in Tandra quizzed them orally. Michael did almost as well as Judy and Jeremy in most of these examinations, but the day Alan tested them about their relations with Mirrorvaxan life, he found that he again would not give the kind of answers Alan wanted. When he and Alan disagreed, Judy sneered at him; and when the session finished, she laughed and called him recyclage in a sharp whisper.

"She always calls you recyclage," Jeremy said when they were both in the egg under the stars. "Why?"

Michael explained how he had been chosen for the mission, how he had been Government stock, and how, indeed, he had been resold and was therefore, as Judy had called him, recyclage.

"But recyclage is a cruel word. And in your case it is not altogether accurate," Jeremy said, without looking at Michael. He jabbed at a button and watched the simulator screen move the pattern of stars a few degrees to the left. "And I can see," he added in a voice that Michael could scarcely hear, "that the name hurts you."

Michael lifted his chin and frowned. "I cannot be hurt," he said. "This isn't Old Vax," he went on, almost angrily. "This is not a child-bearing suburb where we can think of things such as pleasantness and unpleasantness. This is the heart of Transvax, and we are living in the golden age of Vax, when no one is hurt except accidentally—"

Without replying, Jeremy put a hand to his throat.

Michael, seeing him unconvinced, continued, "Of course some people are hurt when the Conglomerates vie for power. But no one means for them to be hurt. All of us are a part of Transvax, and any harm that comes to us comes to Transvax. Transvax—and parts of it, like Judy— only hurt us when they want to make us better or keep us

57

from hurting ourselves. You of all people should realize that."

"You have just admitted," Jeremy replied, "that Judy *did* hurt you. But you mustn't let her, Michael. And you mustn't ever try to hurt her back. She hurts you only because she herself is hurt."

"This is all nonsense," Michael said.

"It is truth," Jeremy said. "Listen, Michael. You must understand why Judy wants to hurt you; why from that very first day she has mocked you and rejected you. You must understand."

"*You* have to understand that I am not hurt," Michael retorted. "Do you think it matters to me what she says or thinks? No! Both of us are parts of the being of Transvax, the person of Transvax. And a person never intentionally hurts himself!"

"You don't understand people if you say that," Jeremy said, his voice edging on brittleness. "You misunderstand what Transvax is, too. But most of all you misjudge Judy. She means her taunt about recyclage to hurt you; she is as shrewed as she is intelligent. She knows what she is doing."

"Why are you telling me this? What does it matter?"

"It matters that you realize why Judy will not accept you."

"Judy must accept me," Michael said.

"Judy," Jeremy said, almost choking on the words, "cannot forget the man you replaced. She cannot forget Mark."

Michael felt the words penetrate his mind, but he told himself they meant nothing. What Jeremy had said might have been true in ancient Vax or in the child-bearing suburbs, but it was far beneath the Space Operations Corporation and its disciplined personnel. It was simply ridiculous. Jeremy, he could see now, was still the brilliant but deluded man he had been before; he had learned nothing from Transvax's mercy. And it was useless to argue with him. Michael closed his ears and forced all that Jeremy had said from his mind. He fixed his eyes on his control panel and pretended to adjust the course.

They did not use the simulator again. The Director, whom Michael had seen only occasionally at the complex, returned to supervise the last steps of their training. The final few days were packed with briefings, tests, and lectures; and even if Michael had wanted to talk to Jeremy, he had no time. And since Jeremy avoided looking at him, Michael felt he had won their argument in the egg.

Only when Judy glared at him, and when on the last night before the flight his nightmare returned, did he begin to doubt it.

BLUE SPACE

THE CONTROL CABIN of *The Arm of Transvax* was exactly like the training simulator. The two seats, in a reclining position, faced the same spectrum of instruments and chattering computers, and Michael's hands, now gloved in layered aluminum, rested near familiar levers and buttons. Curving above him and Jeremy, even the viewscreen seemed to be the same, except that projected on it instead of simulated stars was the face of the Director. He spoke to them above the vibration of the ship and above the distant hiss of escaping steam on the launchpad.

"We now have only a few minutes before countdown sequence," he said, his face distorted by the curve of the screen. "Airspace in this area is clear, atmospheric conditions are ideal, and our launch technicians say a fifth check shows all systems operative and ready." A slight echo of the Director's voice heard through the hatch below him told Michael that Judy, strapped in the lower cabin, was witnessing the same broadcast. "I am tempted at this time," the Director went on, "to remind you of the objectives of the mission and of the precautions you must take to make it a success. But you have all learned your lessons well; we are pleased with your progress and preparation and hope that none of what you have learned will escape you. Remember, above all, that you are the arm of Transvax—"

Michael jumped a little as he saw, from the corner of his eye, the counter to his left begin to register descending digits. He closed his glove on the guidance stick and glanced at Jeremy, who was lifting his helmet over his head. Realizing that he had almost forgotten this step in the lift-off sequence, Michael snatched up his helmet, buckled it on, and began checking instruments through the dark glass of his visor. Meanwhile the Director's voice spoke on in his helmet: "In twenty days you will reach our planet's shadow world, Mirrorvax, which you will investigate and claim for Transvax. You are the tools of Transvax's future—"

"Keep calm," Jeremy's voice cut in. "Remember, the computer does most of the work as long as we are within communication range with Tandra."

Michael nodded but braced his feet and checked the grid of the radar scanner; for the moment it was empty and unmoving. The Director's speech continued, but voices crackled in the background to obscure it. "You three have lived to see the morning of destiny; you three are designed to be instruments of destiny for yourselves, for the Space Operations Corporation, and for Transvax itself. I add my commendation to that of all the Secretariat you saw on tape this morning—you will be remembered as the greatest of all Transvax assets if you succeed."

The Director's face faded away to a view of the AOT from the Flats; the rocket was silhouetted against the morning sun through rising clouds of steam. "Launch sequence, final phase," a voice buzzed. The digits on the counter began to change more rapidly. Static flooded through the audio channels as the rocket engines activated with a roar, and a slight blur of red appeared on the bottom of the broadcast rocket. Michael stiffened. "Steady," Jeremy said. "Launch systems locked in and escalating," another voice said. The roar increased. Michael saw his hand shaking with the increased vibration; he gulped down fear. "Launch condition green plus one," the voice said; "Launch in ten seconds." Green lights beside the screen began flashing. The red stripe of fire beneath the rocket widened. "Launch condition blue minus one," the voice said; "Launch in five seconds." Michael's training, the thousand details about space suits and policies and life-forms, blossomed in his head like the flame beneath the rocket. "Launch blue; systems go; engines fire!"

With a flash of scarlet light, the rocket on the screen edged upward. Red-black flames billowed out, swallowing the launch pad and the empty ground around it, climbing the steel rigging of the towers, obscuring the Space Operations Corporation star on the rocket's lower stage. Michael found himself pinned to his seat; the breath was held in his body as the rocket on the screen gained momentum and lifted upward with an accompanying howl of thunder. Computers glittered overhead. Jeremy growled something to ground control. The *AOT* lurched away from its towers, which automatically fell away, as if drowned by fire from its tail. It climbed upward, and then, with a jolt of added thrust soared heavenward, a diminishing spark of silver marked with a golden tail.

For a time the gravitational force on Michael was so great that he could scarcely blink back heavy tears and move his hand to check thrust systems. The voices from the ground were fainter now, but he heard the launch controller give their altitude and velocity. In moments they would be in the upper atmosphere, and soon after that in space itself. But Michael had no time to absorb his own sense of awe, for soon he had to monitor the thrust balance as the first stage of the rocket disengaged. He watched it fall away on the screen, a smoldering hollow of steel drifting toward the gray-blue curve of Vax below them. The second stage ignited, and Michael watched the features of the world wash away under clouds before he looked at the flight instruments again.

A streak of light caught his eye. Two streaks, two points of light with silver tails. On the radar scanner. They were moving slowly but must have been on the screen for some time, for they had nearly reached its center—the rocket itself. Reflex drove his hand to the course modulation stick, which he shoved forward. The rocket lurched, pitching into a wide arc that made his stomach sink. But only when the computers returned the ship to its course, when the specks of light faded away on the far side of the grid, when the voices began in his helmet, did he realize what he had done. "Ground to AOT. Nice work. You had us scared down here for a while—we lost voice contact. Someone jammed us, the same someone who fired those missiles at you. We're investigating now. Suspect Medron. Hold your course steady and keep your eyes open."

"AOT Michael to ground," he returned. "Course steady. Fuel losses minimal. Narrow scrape."

"Right, AOT Michael. But it shouldn't happen again. Our scans show airspace clear."

"Condition blue, Tandra. Out." Michael switched his voicepath to Jeremy and allowed himself a long sigh. "We almost had a very short flight."

"I . . . I didn't see them coming."

"I didn't either, until they had almost reached us."

"We didn't have much warning," Jeremy said. "The holograph doesn't have much scope for missiles shot from our altitude. It was designed to detect ground-to-air—"

"How did you know the missiles were air-to-air?"

Static answered for a time before Jeremy's voice came on again. "I've been monitering ground control," he said. "The Transvax Air Operations Base at Helcar just shot down a Medron missile shuttle in our area."

The same report had just registered faintly in Michael's earphones. With a sudden and haunting notion, Michael lifted his head and looked at Jeremy, whose face was unreadable beneath his tinted visor. Swallowing abruptly, he settled back in his seat and kept his eyes moving among the instruments. The aft camera showed the Vaxan surface receding beneath them.

After a time, Judy's voice came into his helmet. "We are out of the atmosphere." This seemed at least to lessen the possibility of another missile attack, but Michael found the view on the screen disconcerting. The curve of the planet Vax was clearly visible now. The rear camera also showed the moon edging above the planet's shadow, and the chill even the moon gave him made Michael wonder how he would feel when he at last saw Mirrorvax.

"You should make sure you are secure in your seat," Jeremy's voice said, interrupting Michael's thought. "The second thrust will begin any moment."

A glance at the time counter showed Michael that the second thrust—the burst of force that would snap them out of the gravity field of Vax and accelerate them to their cruising speed—would begin in seconds. He braced himself in time for a noiseless jump of gravitational stress that registered only on the velocity meters and on the aft camera, which after being blinded by a prolonged glow, showed Vax again. The world was only a blue circle now, part pared away in shadow. The thumbnail-sized moon was only a glass bauble in front of a backdrop of black cloth. The vision endured for only a moment, however, because the increasing speed of *The Arm of Transvax* made Vax seem to swallow its moon, then itself sink slowly away to a tiny point of blue light.

"Velocity now stabilizing," Jeremy said, reaching to check gauges all around him. "Course to Mirrorvax set; ground computers yielding vehicular control to ship computers. Tandra reports Vax launch sequence proceeded as anticipated."

"As anticipated," Michael muttered to his visor, watching the radar holograph.

"Cabin pressure returning to habitable limits," Judy's voice said. "Artificial gravity activated. It will be safe enough to take off your helmets and move around in a few minutes. I'll cue you."

Realizing that his seatbelt held him in his seat, not his weight, Michael let one of his arms float free. But already he oriented "down" with the floor of the cockpit, rather than the side. Vax had almost disappeared by the time Judy told them they could take off their helmets.

Michael did so reluctantly, and he quite illogically held his breath for a few moments after he had put his helmet aside. When he began to breathe normally again, he found the air both too thin and too warm. He remained in his seat long after Jeremy stood up and moved into the main cabin. He switched the cameras from aft to forward and watched *The Arm of Transvax* plunge forward into star-speckled darkness. Then, huffing, he gained his feet, steadied himself, and stumped into the main cabin, holding to the door frame for support.

Judy had left her seat, which now was a part of the far wall. She sat at a computer station on what was now the floor, though Michael had always seen it before on a wall; the change dizzied him. Jeremy at a second station was lowering the outer cabin shield. A wide curving window, slowly unsheathed, displayed stars, which, rolling past the spinning spacecraft, made silver streaks on the glass and formed polished-looking clusters beyond. Michael tightened his grip on the door frame. The camera images had not prepared him for his first view of the naked stars. Brilliant dots of fire, they burned paths of flame on the empty horizon; they were so bold, so bright, so beautiful that he drew in a sharp breath.

Judy glared at him. "Awe-stricken?" she said.

Michael released his breath slowly. "Surprised," he said, still watching the stars.

"Surprised?" Judy said. "How?"

"From the simulator films, I thought the stars would be . . . smaller, for one thing. And I expected them to be only faint specks of light—"

"They are only faint specks of light," she interrupted, facing her controls. "And they are no different from what we have seen before."

"But they are!" he retorted, looking to Jeremy for support. "If you don't think so, you are blind. It isn't so much how they look, though; it is more how I feel when I look at them."

Judy laughed. "How you feel?" she said without looking at him. "Michael, you have missed what you would do best in life. You could have saved yourself the shame of becoming recyclage by remaining Government stock. You would have made excellent capital!"

"Judy," Jeremy warned.

"I, capital?" Michael burst out. "By Vax, you are a hypocrite. How can you call *me* capital when you *loved* Mark?"

The fierceness dropped from Judy's face, but anger choked her voice as she whirled toward him in her chair and demanded, "Who told you that?"

"No one had to tell me! I understand now that the reason you . . . attack me is because of *him!*" Michael thumped his thumb against his nametag. "You look at this and see his name, then you look at me and see that I am not him. And you hate me for it!"

"Hate you?" Judy said. Her voice was suddenly icily calm, but the muscles of her face remained tight. "Come now, Michael. Hate is a word our ancestors fabricated. And so is love. If I miss . . . the person you replaced, I miss him only because he was a fine astronaut and a scientist who can never be made up for."

"But I *have* made up for him," Michael said. "The Director himself admitted that I am as well-trained as he would have been."

"The Director," Judy said, lifting her eyes, "lied to you."

"He would have no reason to."

"He does have reason to," Judy said, teeth glittering. "He lied to you to reinforce all of the other lies he has told you—"

"Judy," Jeremy said thickly, "you have said enough."

"What other lies?" Michael asked.

"Judy!" Jeremy repeated.

"I want to know," Michael snapped to Jeremy; then to Judy, "What lies?"

"What truths?" she said, leaning back in her seat. "A few days ago I saw the tape the Director made of his conversation with you in the air-shuttle between Tandra and the Flats and in the complex after you arrived. Just about the only thing he told you that was true was that this mission was going to Mirrorvax and that you were a replacement for Mark—"

"Judy," Jeremy said, "must you?"

"*He* wants the truth," Judy said, watching Michael's frown. "If he wants the truth, I will give it to him. Its sting will be his problem, Jeremy, not yours."

Taking a seat, Michael made his face strong. "I am not afraid of truth where you are concerned, Judy. You use so little of it. And I am not afraid of your 'sting,' either; so I will hear what you have to say."

Judy half-closed her eyes, then laughed. "The truth may be sharper than you think. For the Director did lie to you. He lied to you about how and why you were chosen for this mission. Because you were an advocate? Ha! The Director himself knows well enough that an advocate's only tool is his tongue, and you will not need that on Mirrorvax. Because you fit the spacesuit and could be easily trained? Not really. There were at least a thousand other men—hundreds of them already with Transvax—who could have worn that suit and learned those lessons."

Michael shifted in his seat. "Why was I chosen, then?"

"Because you were the right size and trainable, in part. But the Director bought you—and most likely had someone leak his plans to buy you to Syntac—so that he would have a third astronaut who was incredibly in his debt. Jeremy and I have been with this project so long that the Director can not still manipulate us, though he still assumes he can. But

67

he trusts neither of us completely. Little more than he trusted Mark or any of the alternates. He arranged their deaths by another information leak to Medron. He may have wanted to kill Jeremy and me as well, but we seemed to be loyal, and he had no time to instruct new astronauts and still meet his schedule. And those he trained might learn to be as scornful of Transvax as we, anyway. So he bought you. In you he wanted loyalty—two thousand chronas worth. He did not necessarily want skill. Jeremy and I have enough of that."

Michael stormed to his feet. "That isn't true! You lied when you said the Director wanted Mark dead! The Director is more logical than that. Why would he destroy what he had worked to create? You are mistaken, Judy. You must be. Isn't she, Jeremy?"

Jeremy had been facing him, but he turned his chair toward a computer panel. He let his fingers play across the keyboard. "Ground control, this is AOT Jeremy requesting revised flight information."

Without looking away from Michael, Judy folded her arms and stretched out her legs. He knew he must be turning red. He backed away, then dived into the cockpit, where, away from her stare, he managed to sort out his thoughts. She was wrong, he knew. But even if she were right, would it be so terrible? What mattered was that he had done what was expected of him so far. He had done more than was expected of him, in fact. His task now was to repay the Director his debt, no matter how the debt had come to be.

The camera view of the endless stars told him that he was indeed on his way to Mirrorvax. That was the one important thing. And if the only quality he was prized for was his loyalty, he would make sure the mission would not fail.

As soon as they finished a round of instrument checks, they began the routine of their flight. Two crewmembers were to be awake and at the controls; the third was to sleep The duty shifts were to revolve so that each of them slept one third of the time—in an air-tight sleeping compartment off the main cabin—and man the instruments, eat, and exercise for two-thirds of the time. Michael slept first; rather, he lay in the noiseless sleeping compartment for a long time, staring at the ceiling. He reached sleep, or so it seemed, just before Jeremy awakened him.

The first shift with Judy was hard, for she persisted in staring at him, even when he was eating or jogging on the treadmill by the windows. Michael found communication with the ground pleasant, for it gave him the chance to concentrate on the instruments and on the static-smudged voice in his earphones.

When Judy traded off with Jeremy, Michael thought things would be more pleasant. But Jeremy avoided talking to him; and because the voices of ground control grew fainter and came less frequently, Michael became bored. He almost wished the shipboard computers were not so capable. They left him with little more to do than to glance between stable instruments and stare at the shift of the stars beyond the viewport. He dropped to sleep in a few moments on his second visit to the sleeping compartment.

The shifts, though they never seemed to go faster, blurred together. Michael found himself checking the chronometers to see how many days away from Mirrorvax they were. He came to loathe their packaged nutrients, even though he had eaten nothing else since his arrival at the Flats. He came to dread Judy and Jeremy equally and look forward to the privacy of his sleep, only to find them waiting in dreams. Wakening always to the same metallic cabin and the same fierce stars, he began to feel as if he had never known anything else, as if he would live like this forever. Only when occasional taped messages from the Director came did he recall the magnitude of his mission and realize that—very soon—he would see Mirrorvax.

One sleeping period Michael awoke sweating and emerged

into the main cabin to find the window-shield down and Jeremy and Judy busy at the controls. Sniffing the air, he realized the reason for the heat that had awakened him; they had now cut past the orbit of Phoros into the sun's inner radiation and gravitational field. From the chronometer he saw that time had passed for Judy to take his place. But when he told her, she refused to leave her seat and continued shouting status readings to Jeremy, who worked navigational controls furiously, his face sweat-dotted, his teeth set. All Michael could do was sit down and watch the instruments register gravitational winds. He heard the whine of strained engines and felt jolts from power shifts and gravitational wind. He brought food and water to Jeremy and Judy, all the while soaking moisture from his face with a cloth. Yet he sweated less from the heat than from uneasiness.

"I can spell one of you off!" he shouted over the vibration of the ship after another sleep period had passed. "I know what to do."

"If this mission has to end, I don't want the ship to go by plunging into the sun!" Jeremy returned. "Let's all stay where we are."

By the end of another sleeping period, the cabin had cooled to normal temperature, and the image of the sun on their scanners grew smaller. The shrill of the engines heard through the walls of the ship died away. The digits on the meters gradually returned to their customary levels. At last Judy, raw-eyed, consented to sleep, and as soon as she had gone into the sleeping compartment, Jeremy lowered himself from his chair, sat on the floor, and motioned for Michael to take his seat. "Things look stable now," he said. "The ship should run itself, even now that we are out of contact with ground control. But if anything looks funny, wake me up." He stretched out on his side, dropped his head on his arm, and half-closed his eyes. Pressing his lips, Michael threw himself into Jeremy's seat and glared at the controls. He jabbed at a button, then glared at Jeremy.

"It isn't that we didn't trust you," Jeremy said.

"Oh, it's not?" Michael hunched over the console. "It's just that you trusted yourselves more, right?"

"You might say that," Jeremy muttered. "Passing the sun was, after all, the most dangerous part of our voyage. This spacecraft is almost perfectly designed, Michael; it is such a wonder of technology that it could almost pilot itself to Mirrorvax and back without us. The only times that anything could go wrong is when we are in a planet's or the sun's gravitational field. In fact, the only way any of us could stop this mission from being a success is by sending this ship into the sun or toward a planet, where it would burn up in the atmosphere or crash on the surface."

"I will remember that if I want to destroy the ship."

"Remember that even if you don't," Jeremy said. "If there are hostile life-forms that could use this ship to go back across space to harm Vax, one of us would have to destroy the ship. One of us would have to burn it up in the Mirrorvaxan atmosphere."

"That wasn't in the training packet," Michael said, narrowing his eyes at Jeremy. "But it sounds well worked-out. Is it an idea of your own?"

"You are missing the whole point," Jeremy said. "I was trying to point out the dangers of passing the sun. We just could not have taken any risks—"

"If you had 'taken no risks'—if you had kept me from the controls during lift-off—none of us would be here now," Michael said. "*I* saved us from the Medron missiles, remember? Or do you regret that I did? You know, I think you saw those missiles before I did."

"I . . . I didn't see them at all," Jeremy said.

"I think you did. And what is more, I think you jammed our contact with ground control just so they couldn't warn us."

"That's absurd!"

"Maybe you even told Medron the time of our launch!"

Jeremy laughed; his laugh was half-throated and very dry.

71

It sounded like paper being wadded. "Maybe Judy is right when she says you should have been capital. You have the imagination for it. Now, why in the name of Vax would I want to have Medron missiles destroy us?"

"That's what I would like to know," Michael said.

"If I wanted this ship destroyed, for whatever reason you fancy, why did I rescue it from the sun's gravity?"

"I don't know," Michael said, looking at the controls. "But I know something isn't right." His voice softened as he turned his chair to face Jeremy. "I'm a little scared, that's all. I *know* you saw those missiles on the holograph before I did. I know that much."

The shadows deepened around Jeremy's mouth. "If I . . . hesitated," he said in a voice so low that Michael could scarcely hear it, "it was only because I glimpsed a simple way to put an end to the Director's scheming."

"To Transvax's scheming," Michael corrected, suddenly beginning to understand. "You still hate Transvax for what they did to you, don't you? You still can't accept—"

"Justice? Do you still call it justice, Michael?"

"I am Transvax. What else could I call it?"

Jeremy did not answer for a long time. "I want you to understand one thing, Michael. I don't really want to wreck this ship at the expense of your life and Judy's. You saw how fiercely I fought the sun to keep us all alive. By Vax, Michael, do you think I have no feeling?"

"All of us would do better to have no feeling," Michael snapped. "Feelings are primitive things that animals and people in child-bearing suburbs have. When they begin to interfere with the workings of such tools of the Conglomerate as you and me, it's dangerous for us all."

"It's time we became dangerous, then," Jeremy said. "But you have nothing to fear from me. If that will put you at ease."

Choosing not to answer, Michael activated the long-range radioscope and played with the dials until a tiny speck of light focused in the center of the screen. "Mirrorvax," he said, grinning as the dot of light sharpened, "it's now"—he ran his finger along the instrument panel—"four Vaxan days away!"

"Four days and forever," Jeremy said.

"What was that?"

"Forever," Jeremy said. "All three of us will meet with destiny in four days—isn't that what the Director says?"

"Yes," Michael said. "But the Director also says that only the arms of Transvax will reach out to Destiny. Anything that goes to Mirrorvax by itself . . . for itself . . . is liable to meet Fate."

"The Director said nothing of the kind—though you said it rather well yourself. I shudder to think this, but I am beginning to think that Judy is right after all. About the reasons the Director wanted you to go to Mirrorvax."

FREEFALL

MIRRORVAX FIRST APPEARED in the forward camera as just another star, and a faint one at that. Surrounded by brighter points of fire, it seemed insignificant and drab, and Michael felt somehow disappointed. But Judy, with whom he was working when they both first saw it, grinned and sighted all her scanning instruments toward it; the object, she told him excitedly, did seem to be a planet. Because no scientists had ever seen Mirrorvax, there had been a touch of doubt that it existed or that it was indeed a world. Some scientists had conjectured that it could be a large asteroid or possibly even a tear in space or a shadow of the world Vax, ruled by none of the physical laws that held true elsewhere in the universe.

"That much, at least, is comforting," Michael said. But he had never really expected anything else. He found it hard to mirror Judy's enthusiasm.

When Judy woke him at the end of his next sleeping period, he found Mirrorvax had taken on new prominence in the forward screen; it glittered, the size of an air-shuttle landing light, blinding the stars around it. Jeremy said he thought its light was tinted with green, but after gazing at it, Michael thought it looked blue, very much the color

Vax had seemed from a similar distance. Peering at her instruments, Judy told them that from her best calculations, Mirrorvax was a world very near the size of Vax. It probably had some kind of atmosphere, though it was really too early to judge.

Michael took her station when she went into the compartment to sleep. He toyed with the spectrograph and some of the other instruments, but he was most interested in the view through the forward telescope, in which Mirrorvax was coin-sized, smooth, and definitely blue, threaded perhaps with white. "Oxygen," he said, aiming the spectroscope through the telescope, "and nitrogen, I'm almost sure. This spectrum looks almost like the pattern of light reflected from Vax. That means—"

"That Mirrorvax was not an inaccurate name," Jeremy said, looking at him. "We are getting close enough now to get all kinds of readings on these instruments. And none of them are any different from what they would be if we were approaching Vax."

"Then the theory that Mirrorvax is a reflection world may be right."

"I don't know about that," Jeremy said. "The term *reflection* gets sticky when you think about it. If Mirrorvax is an *exact* copy of Vax, that could mean that at this very moment our counter-selves on a counter-spacecraft are taking readings of Vax and wondering the same things we are. No, I don't think it is a *mirror*-world. I think instead that it is a *twin* world, a world of the same proportions and makeup, but of different geography and history. The universe never repeats itself exactly. But maybe it often works with the same mold."

Michael glanced at the forward screen; there Mirrorvax was almost as big as it had been in the telescope only a few minutes before. "I see what you mean. And I somehow think you're right. At least I hope you are right. Something about that mirror idea makes me uneasy."

"It's disconcerting to think there might be another version of myself," Jeremy said.

"That isn't what bothers me," Michael said, blinking back a mental picture of himself wearing a sinister smile. "But the thought that at this very moment *their* ship could be approaching Vax—"

"They wouldn't do anything to Vax that we wouldn't do to Mirrorvax."

"That," Michael said, "is exactly what I'm afraid of. For instance—"

"We are starting to feel Mirrorvaxan gravity," Jeremy broke in. "We will snap into orbit before too long. Maybe you had better wake Judy."

"I can handle her station."

"That isn't the point," Jeremy said. "We will need all three of us to make a landing. We have to start landing procedures right away, because we don't have fuel enough to make more than a single orbit."

Michael frowned. "We were supposed to have fuel enough for ten."

"Supposed," Jeremy said. "Things have changed since launch. You used fuel to dodge those missiles, remember? And we used more fuel than we expected when we went past the sun—"

"But right here the fuel meters say—"

"The fuel meters are jammed," Jeremy snapped. "They must be. The sun's heat must have broken them. They haven't moved since we left the sun's radiation field. I've calculated our fuel use, and I'm sure they're off. Or would you like to take ten orbits and risk not having enough fuel to get back to Vax?"

"All right," Michael said, a little puzzled. "But won't it be difficult to decide on a landing site in only one orbit?"

"That's why I want you to wake Judy now. *Now,* Michael."

Judy seemed irritated when Michael touched her arm, but when she caught sight of the sparkling globe on the forward screen, she pushed past him and took her station.

Soon she told them readings that confirmed what Jeremy had said before; in the large sense, Mirrorvax was a copy of Vax. Its atmosphere seemed Vaxlike—close enough, Judy asserted, that they would probably be able to breathe it once they had checked for bacteria. Its gravity matched Vax's; and it even had a moon, visible like a bit of aluminum on the far left of the screen. But as Mirrorvax grew nearer, Judy's reports changed. "That moon is less than half the size of our own, and its orbit is tighter. It has irregularities on it I can read from here—it's practically an asteroid. There are hints, too, that there may be another moon we can't see. Keep an eye on your radar holograph, Jeremy. Let's not have a sudden crash landing into the dark side of something. Isn't our velocity a little high?"

"The main engines are off," Jeremy said. "I'm bringing her in more sharply than we had planned—to save fuel. We're coasting now, with help from Mirrorvax's gravity."

Michael was scarcely listening. He stood in the middle of the cabin, eyes fixed on the growing globe on the screen. Its shadow made it oblong, but the sunlit part of it flamed in glimmering blue-belted in clouds. He fancied he could see the outlines of landforms now, of broad rectangular continents under the atmosphere. As he examined Mirrorvax, the divisions of water and land, as he saw them, grew more clear in his mind. Tracing the curve of the world down from the polar cap, he isolated two distinct continents and a large island between them. Over one continent clouds were thick, but the other was laid bare to him. The part of it he could see was triangular; from its irregular north coast a peninsula protruded like a hand. Jeremy and Judy were still arguing about whether Mirrorvax had oceans or not, but perhaps because Michael saw more through the camera than they saw through their instruments, he knew that it did. He knew also, without a look at Judy's computer, that the planet would have life; but when Judy told them that was unlikely, he did not argue with her, for his only proof was an odd feeling—not the kind of feeling he

77

had always called primitive before, but a piercing and almost frightening realization. The only time he had experienced anything similar was once when he had looked at the reflection of a man for a long time before understanding that the man was himself.

He started at a touch on his arm. "You can stare later," Jeremy said, guiding him toward the cockpit. "Right now we had better belt ourselves in. We'll be entering orbit in a matter of moments."

As soon as Michael had strapped himself into his seat and clamped on his helmet, he heard Judy's voice in his earphones. "I am deactivating cabin gravity now, and I don't think I'll be able to keep cabin pressure steady, so keep your helmets on. We have reached orbit."

"Orbit status," Jeremy's voice buzzed in. "Locking into an elliptical path that will take us over four of the seven continents. We have good altitude now, but we may not be able to keep it for long. Engines seem sluggish. But unless the engines die, Michael, don't switch to our alternate reserves. We'll need those for the home journey."

"Right," Michael said, though his fuel gauge still registered far from empty.

The surface of Mirrorvax now reared up in front of them, filling the screen with white-veined blue. Michael stretched forward in his seat, for he fancied he saw a hand-shaped peninsula moving toward them. "Where will we land?" he asked, opening a channel to Jeremy.

But before Jeremy could answer, Judy's voice cut in. "The computer has now given me five possible coordinates for landing sites, all of them in our path of orbit, all of them on apparently level areas near the sea. I'm having the computer select the prime location from data now coming in from other instruments."

Jeremy's glove curled around the course modulation stick. "I want you to reprogram the computer," he said suddenly. Michael saw him stiffen. "I hope you can do it quickly."

"Reprogram the computer? To do what?"

78

"To find a landing site further inland," Jeremy said. "And a site within half an orbit of here, if you can. Don't argue with me, Judy. Just do what I say, unless you fancy a water landing. We are so short on fuel that we won't be able to maneuver much when we drop into the atmosphere, so we can't risk hitting water. That is one eventuality this ship is not equipped to meet."

"Jeremy," Michael said, watching Mirrorvax unfold beneath him, "do you think that is wise?"

"It is more than wise. It is imperative. Judy, can you adjust the programming?"

"I'm trying," she answered. Her voice, suddenly, seemed remote.

"But we can't land inland," Michael said. "Jeremy, that's against our orders. The scientists said it was essential to be near an ocean, if there was any, because life would be more likely to thrive there—"

"At this point," Jeremy returned gruffly, "I am more concerned about *our* lives than about any life on this planet. By Vax, have you forgotten our fuel situation?"

"And how do you assume that our 'fuel situation' warrants breaking orders when my gauge says we have enough to orbit ten times, to take our time landing, never having to switch to auxiliary fuel? How can you justify an emergency landing when all of my instruments disagree with you?"

"I'm the commander, Michael. You just have to trust me."

Michael seized the course modulation stick. "I don't trust you, Jeremy. I don't see how you can say we are short on fuel. And you're not the commander. The Director is the commander, his his orders were—"

"Blast the Director, and blast his orders! You would follow instructions until this ship burned to a cinder running out of fuel in the atmosphere!"

"*You* would ram it into a mountain, just to punish Transvax. I can't let you disobey orders unless you can give me proof about the fuel supply!"

"I don't have time to give you proof!"

"Yes you do," Michael said. "We have ten orbits. By Vax, I'm not going to let you take us down yet!"

"And how will you stop me?" Jeremy said. "How are you going to report me to the Director with the sun standing between us and Vax?"

"I don't need the Director to stop you!" Michael said. He lunged forward, meaning to tear Jeremy's hand from the course modulation stick, but his strappings held him back.

"Both of you stay calm up there," Judy's voice said, washed-over with increasing static. "I can't tell what the level of the fuel supply is. I don't have time to make calculations. But I have a landing spot, Jeremy. Just one. The only place clear of cloud cover, away from the sea, and in our immediate path of orbit." She gave Jeremy coordinates, which he entered into the navigation computer. "But I can't guess what the terrain will be like. My program isn't as thorough as the one that is built in. And we haven't had time to make proper surveys. Jeremy—"

Switching her voice channel off, Jeremy steadied himself in his seat. Michael shouted something to him, but he did not turn his head; Michael guessed Jeremy had turned off his earphones. "He's mad," Michael said, patching through to Judy. "Jeremy's mad!" The odd words Jeremy had spoken in the egg came back, and Michael felt suddenly dizzy. "I think he means to drop us into a mountainside!"

"Even if that happens," Judy said, "I don't think it will be Jeremy's fault. He isn't mad—after all, if we are short on fuel—"

"If!" Michael roared.

"We'll have to trust him and hope for the best . . ." Her voice seemed to fade away. "Whatever our fuel situation was, we've halved our distance to the surface in the last few minutes, and to pull away now would tax even our auxiliary tanks. Michael, we're dropping fast, and we're about to hit the outer—" the ship jolted "—atmosphere."

The surface of Mirrorvax loomed now over the whole

screen; its clouds were broad, its oceans glittering far to the right. Below, a featureless swath of gray was fast sharpening into detail as the digits on the altimeter dropped. Michael thought he saw markings, paths of rivers, perhaps, or ranges of mountains. Mountains. He cried out Jeremy's name, but Jeremy, clenching the course modulation stick, entered constant numbers into the navigation computer. The edges of the camera view fogged with heat. The jagged features of mountain ranges and river-cut gorges, for a moment all too clear, blurred away into a red-tinted smear. Smelling heated metal, Michael contacted Judy, but she was already shouting, perhaps to Jeremy: "Skin temperature is reaching a critical point! You must fire the thrusters to slow us down!"

Jeremy only edged back on the stick; wind screamed against the hull of the ship. It grew hotter, even inside Michael's suit. The screen flared red and then went dark. Instruments flickered with wild numbers. The engines moaned. Something struck against the wall not far from Michael. "Pull back!" Judy's voice shrilled, threaded with static. "Jeremy, fire the landing thrusters."

"Jeremy can't hear you," Michael barked. "But I can!" Groping for the control panel, he jabbed black buttons, three of them, then finally the fourth. A noise like thunder swallowed his ears, the cockpit shook, and the body of the ship shuddered. Michael was sure it would buckle, but as the hiss of the reverse thrusters continued, the digits on the gauges slowed, and gravity suddenly dragged against him, snapping him forward, hanging him in his strappings. Jeremy's voice imprinted itself on his confusion: "Not thrusters now, Michael! We don't have the fuel! We have to wait until the last moment!"

"This *was* the last moment!" Michael huffed, but then the vibrating roar of the thrusters peaked, hesitated, then with a rattling explosion ceased. Michael, suddenly slammed back into his seat, knew that the thrusters had failed and that they were now falling freely.

"The fuel, it's gone!" Jeremy shouted. "Yield me control

of the thrusters! And switch to the auxiliary fuel pods. You've squandered the last of our main supply!"

Dumbfounded, Michael gaped at the blank fuel gauge, then shifted control to Jeremy, who, red-faced, took the course modulation stick and glared at the digits piling up on the meters. He bit his lip as heat began again to build in the cockpit, and just when Michael thought again that Jeremy might be trying to destroy the ship, he tore the stick backwards and an instant later activated the forward thrusters. The ship pitched, tumbled over itself, and then with a mammoth groan stabilized nose up. The forward thrusters wheezed on until the ship lurched almost to a standstill.

"Now comes the hard part," Jeremy rasped.

"The hard part?"

"Landing blind," Jeremy answered. He shot a glance at Michael. "At least, thank Vax, there's less chance of hitting water. I knew that our fuel-efficient entry would cost us our vision—that's why I had Judy plot those new coordinants—I didn't want to hit the sea. Now, I don't have any idea of what's just below us, no more than you do. It may be, as you said, a mountainside. But we can't waste any more fuel—as it is we may not have enough to get back to Vax."

Michael looked at the thruster buttons, but wondered still what would have happened if he hadn't slowed the ship. They could have burned up.

"I'm going to set her down now," Jeremy said. He began to decrease thrust bit by bit. Michael could feel the ship settling downward.

"I don't have any radar information for you," Judy's voice hissed. "The scanner must have burned away in entry. It's giving me jagged pictures."

The roar of the engines began to die away. The base of the rocket touched something, and downward movement stopped. But when Jeremy cut back the engines, emptiness opened beneath them, and the ship slammed downward. When Michael regained his senses, he found that the cockpit rested slantwise, tilting slightly to the right. And though the engines had died and the control lights blinked only feebly, he heard flames somewhere below him, brittle-sounding flames snapping and crackling against the hull.

"Judy," Michael said into his visor microphone, "is there a fire down there?"

Static answered for a long time before her voice came. "Not inside the ship. I'm going to open the view panel—it's opening only a little—heat from our entry must have melted it shut." A pause followed, then a gasp. "Great Vax, there's a fire out there. Something's burning."

"Burning?" Jeremy asked. "What's on fire?"

Judy hesitated. Then she said, "Trees."

PART
2

THE FOREVER
MOUNTAINS

JUDY HAD SENT a can-sized plastic cylinder through a specially designed airlock, and when she brought it back in, she checked to make sure the seal had set, then fitted it into a circular aperture in her analysis computer. It dropped out of sight, and only a moment later data began to appear to a read-out screen.

Jeremy, meanwhile, stood beside a screen of his own, a big lighted wall panel on which several red dots flashed at junctions of black lines. He followed the system paths with his little finger, noting the location of malfunction lights, measuring the extent of damage with a deepening frown. "It is bad," he said at last, "but it could be worse. We can repair most of the damage, though it may take time and ingenuity."

Standing beside the open slit in the view panel, Michael bowed his head; though their fuel shortage had caused their sudden landing, he himself had fired the reverse thrusters and used some of the last of the fuel, so in a way he felt responsible for at least some of the system breakdowns Jeremy was now noting. He grimaced. He lifted one hand to the edge of the vertical window and peered through the heat-smeared glass toward the outside. Only now were the smoke and steam clearing enough to let him see.

Directly below him, around the base of the ship, soot-colored flatness steamed, marked as his eyes roamed outward by stubble and knobs of still-flaming debris. Perhaps fifty meters away from the ship charred stumps and trunks were still burning, and further beyond (though it was hard to tell because of the smoke) was a charred horizon of trees, conifers perhaps, and beyond that a hint of pale blue sky smudged by smoke and billowing steam. The scene looked something as it might have if *The Arm of Transvax* had landed in a food-production orchard, though the trees on the horizon seemed far more irregular and twisted-looking.

Without looking away from the Mirrorvaxan surface, Michael opened the wall locker and took out a translator device, which he dangled for a moment in his fingers, letting it catch Mirrorvaxan daylight. "We might need these, after all," he said in a low voice. He put it on.

"Don't even *think* of that possibility now," Jeremy said.

"I can't help it." Michael fixed the tiny audiophone to his ear. "After all, if there are trees that look so much like those on Vax—"

Jeremy shook his head slowly for an answer. He entered some figures from the wall panel into a nearby computer.

"Hm," Judy said, hunching over her console. "This air sample has an unusual number of carbon compounds. But those can be accounted for because of the smoke and the engine fumes. If I adjust my calculations for that, this air seems perfectly Vaxan. Perfectly." She produced a second cylinder and pressed it into the airlock. "But I'd better take another sample."

"If we can breathe the air, the repairs on the outside of the ship will be easy, and we won't have to tax our oxygen supplies," Jeremy said. "If your second sample gives us the same results, we'll go out unpressurized. *With filters*, that is. We can't forget about bacteria."

"Or higher forms of life," Michael said.

"Most of the bacteria in the immediate area of the ship,"

Judy broke in, as if changing the subject, "will have been sterilized anyway."

Jeremy turned away from his panel to watch Judy make calculations on her new sample of air. When she turned around and nodded to him, he folded his arms. "One of us should go out," he said.

"I am the science crewmember," Judy said, lifting her head. "I should go. Besides," she added, glancing down at her hands, "if I am in error with my calculations, I should be the one to pay the price."

"I trust your calculations," Jeremy said. "I will go, because I am the commander and ought to be the first to walk on the planet Mirrorvax."

"I am most . . . expendable," Michael said uneasily. "I should go."

"If we are thinking in terms of expendability, I should go, since as science crewmember I am least necessary to the actual functioning of the ship," Judy said. "Only you know how to repair the ship, Jeremy, and both you and Michael ought to be in the cockpit when we blast off again. Though I do think," she said, with something almost like a sneer, "it is hardly a matter of life and death."

Jeremy considered, then finally dipped his head toward her. "But see that you take no chances." He glanced at her. "Let me go down to the cargo cabin and bring you a pressure suit."

"The air is like Vaxan air. I don't need a suit."

"I insist that you at least wear a filter," Jeremy said.

"A filter, certainly. Until I can take readings on bacteria."

"You ought to take a translator, too," Michael said.

Judy laughed. "Why? To talk to the bacteria or to the trees?"

In a few minutes Judy declared she was ready. She wore the same space suit she had worn at launch, but equipment slung over her shoulder and strapped to her waist almost hid it. Several death-coils were looped over her free arm, and a cylinder of Medron venom-eggs swayed from a hook on her belt. Most of her face was hidden by her gauze filter mask, and her fierce eyes burning above it made her look like an ancient veiled empress of Vax. She did not speak as they descended the ladder to the lower cargo hold and paused at the elevator-airlock to see her out.

By the time Michael and Jeremy climbed back to the cabin and the view panel, Judy had already emerged below. She was stooping in the ash a few paces from the ship, testing its texture with a gloved finger. Her dark hair, falling past her face, stirred slightly in the Mirrorvaxan wind. When she straightened, she saw them and waved. Michael imagined she was smiling beneath the filter, and seeing her standing in the sunlight, he suddenly wished he had argued his position more strongly.

"We should have given her a radio so she could talk to us," Michael said.

Jeremy squinted through the glass. "For being so fond of the Director's regulations, you forget them quickly," he said. " 'You shall use no short-wave communication devices, unless absolutely necessary, until you have determined the level of the technology of the Mirrorvaxan inhabitants, if any.' It wouldn't be smart, if there is any kind of advanced civilization in Mirrorvax, to let them know about us before we know about them."

"If there are any intelligent creatures here at all," Michael retorted, "they will have seen us dropping or at least the smoke from the crash. I hope you warned Judy not to go too far."

"I did. But I don't foresee any danger. Even if someone did see us, it will take them a long time to reach us. My radar scan shows that we are, as you thought we might be, on a mountainside."

Judy, meanwhile, was moving away from the flame-leveled ground toward the first charred trees. Her progress was slow, for she often stopped to take readings or to kneel in the ash and take samples. She did not look back at them, and as soon as she reached the first unburned trees, she turned and started moving along them, picking leaves and rubbing them between her fingers, tucking twigs into her knee pockets, holding her instruments up in the wind. Soon she disappeared from view. Michael pushed his face against the glass, trying in vain to catch another glimpse of her. She had moved too far out of sight.

"That's that," Jeremy said. "Judy will be back before long with a packet of samples and a dozen theories. In the meantime, you and I had better start on repairs."

Michael moaned. After envying Judy's first moments of discovery, he felt disappointed, but he followed Jeremy to the systems panel and listened to a description of the work they would undertake in the next few days. He clenched his teeth when they descended to the cargo deck and began opening crates in search of spare parts. He consented to read code numbers off boxes to Jeremy, for he remembered that to assist Jeremy was one of his duties. And he felt he needed to make up for igniting the thrusters.

By the time they began rerouting wiring systems, Judy still had not returned. Sitting cross-legged on the floor, fishing plastic-covered parts from the box for Jeremy, Michael wondered how far she had gone. Maybe far enough to see what lay beyond the trees, to take the first glimpse of the wild Mirrorvaxan landscape.

Next he and Jeremy assembled cameras to replace the ones that had burned off the hull. They would position them when Judy gave them more information about the planet, Jeremy told him. "But hasn't she been gone a long time?" Michael said when he had fitted a lens onto the second camera. "Shouldn't she be back by now?"

Jeremy checked the chronometer. "Scientists are thorough," he said. "And it hasn't been that long. Don't get fingerprints on the lens, if you can help it."

They soon set the cameras aside and began work on a short-barreled piece of artillery especially designed to be carried. Michael thought the components of the thing had a sinister look: the long metal tube, the miniature computer, the black power pack, the heat coils. But it seemed far more cruel once assembled; even if the device had not looked like an unfingered arm stretching from a massive shoulder, it would have reminded him of his auction day, of moaning sounds and explosions of sparks. It reminded him also, though he could not explain why, of the bearded commander of the Transvax auction complex security. What if that man, he thought suddenly, had died only to buy his loyalty?

"Loyalty," he muttered, staring at the short-barrel.

"What was that?"

"It has been a while since Judy left," Michael said. He glanced toward the window. "And there is still no sign of her. Don't you think that one of us ought to check on her? Not that I think anything has happened to her, but she might be busy with something she has found."

Jeremy hesitated, then nodded. "I'll go."

"I'd like to go, if you don't mind," Michael said, standing up. "If we use our old criterion, I am the least valuable—"

"I think it's high time we stopped thinking in those terms," Jeremy said. "As if going through the airlock is certain death. Go ahead, if you want to. And take the short-barrel with you, just to show Judy that we have begun to worry about her. You do know how to fire artillery, don't you?"

Michael held back his anger. "I was fairly good on the practice range."

"Here," Jeremy said, heaving the short-barrel into Michael's arms. "The real test of handling artillery is carrying it. Good luck going down the ladder to the airlock."

Michael did have a troublesome time reaching the cargo deck, and he had to dump the short-barrel on top of a crate while he found a filter. "What if I can't find her near the ship?" he shouted up to Jeremy.

"Look for her a little beyond, but don't go too far. If you have any trouble, come back here."

"Right." The filter muted his reply. After adjusting the filter straps on the back of his neck, he cradled the short-barrel in his arms and opened the inner door of the airlock. He thought, when the seal closed behind him, that the air of the lock smelled of something familiar, but not until the outer door opened did he realize what it was.

Once, when he had been too small to know such things were foolish, he had awakened to specks of moisture on his window. He had left the building and had gone to the walkways, sniffing the smell of rain-wet concrete and morning-cold steel. He had stood under the rain to drink its coolness, to watch it drop into his eyes from the clouds. He remembered this, suddenly, when he took his first breath of Mirrorvaxan air through the door. In spite of the filter, he knew it had recently rained. He smelled ash and burning, too; but those odors seemed faint and fading.

The Mirrorvaxan wind numbed the exposed part of his face as he tapped down the metal boarding stairs. The print of Judy's boots led away in the ash, but he did not put his feet where hers had been. He took several steps on his own, feeling the irregular surface beneath his boots. Then he stopped to take his first real look at Mirrorvax.

Only a few faint smudges of smoke rose now; they twisted and vanished into the wind. The same wind combed through the long branches of trees that circled the burned-away clearing. Some of the trees looked almost Vaxan; some of them could only have been conifers, and some of them looked like fruit trees Michael had seen. But others—tall, spindly trees with frondlike branches and stout, dark green trees with flat tops—looked utterly alien, particularly when the wind moved them. The sky was not as clear as Michael had thought. A veneer of cloud paled it, and directly above, rainclouds gathered; the low slant of the sun made them seem purplish. Through gaps in the trees Michael saw that mountains, too, encroached on the sky. Jagged cliffs on his right seemed far away, but they loomed above the trees with faces of flesh-colored stone. Distant blue peaks pricked up on the far right, fuzzy in the haze, touched at their summits with flecks that could be either stone or snow. Staring from one feature to the next, Michael first gasped, then shuddered, then finally allowed himself a smile beneath his filter. Mirrorvax—at least this part of it—was perfect. Perfect for what Transvax could make it. It was the kind of world Space Corporation scientists dreamed about, the kind of world that would make Transvax master of the solar system. Michael sighed and looked over the scene again. In the near future, these trees would make shelters for the first Transvax colonist. The mountains themselves, no matter how they frowned in their power now, would be mined and quarried and granulated and drilled and dredged and processed until they became part of the New Mirrorvax, the spaceport and industrial base that would develop, perhaps in this very place. Michael could sense already that Mirrorvax was a wild planet, an empty and silent world, as Vax had once been. The first colonists (perhaps he would return and be one of them) would have to battle the mountains and the rains; but bit by bit, they would make Mirrorvax an outpost, then a trading center, then an industrial community, and eventually a complete world.

Much of what the Director had said about destiny came back to Michael. He could not help feeling, no matter what Judy or Michael might say, that he indeed was a small piece of forever. He thought that nothing in his life had ever been quite so important as stepping onto this planet's surface. He closed his eyes and smiled.

The weight of the short-barrel, however, soon reminded him of his task. Shouldering the weapon, he started to cross the ash. Judy's bootprints were not hard to follow, though he found himself sidetracked by the same things that might have interested Judy—a lone leaf wagging on a burned sapling, a charred length of log, an unusual shrub. He found more distractions when he reached the edge of the burned circle, but he did his best to contain his curiosity. He would have time for investigation later.

He had expected to sight Judy not long after he reached the trees. But he saw no sign of her. Her tracks followed the edge of the burn, occasionally straying through clumps of trees or to a growth-covered rock. When Michael glanced up from the trail some time later, he saw that he had rounded half of the rocket's burn—the unwindowed side of the *AOT*, a flame-blackened bullet, was across from him, tilting slightly toward the sun. He had just decided that Judy must have decided simply to make a complete circuit and that she was probably back at the ship, when her tracks ended.

This did not alarm him at first. For the tracks disappeared into a grassy oval flanked by tall fern-trees. But soon he saw they did not emerge again; stalking the shipward side of the oval, he found no more of them. "She took it in her head to go into the forest," he said aloud. But he cocked the short-barrel and raised it as he walked deeper into the oval.

The wind, he noticed for the first time, made an odd keening in the fern-trees. Yet the wind had not one voice but many, each of which found a different pitch. The effect was something like distant sirens. He halted. The movement of the fern-trees suddenly seemed irregular, as if the pale green fronds were fingers, not branches. When one of them brushed him, he swung around, his finger near the activation switch of the short-barrel. Finding nothing there, he chided himself. But he kept his thumb ready as he pressed forward. The *AOT* dropped out of sight behind a tall tangle-covered rock. He could still see the cliffs, but the rock on their walls no longer seemed pale. Shadow and the low sun made them seem orange, and the same odd light made the details of the trees just ahead hard to distinguish.

At the end of the grass, Michael stopped. Keeping the short-barrel propped toward the thicker trees, he knelt and looked at the ground. When he was sure there were no tracks, he returned his eyes to the shadows in the trees.

Only then did he see an oblong of flattened grass; propping the short-barrel against his knee, he squatted to investigate. Something fairly large had fallen there not long before. Judy? But even if Judy had made the imprint, neither she nor any piece of her equipment was there now. Perhaps, he thought, she had only stumbled there. But two bits of color caught his eye at once, and they turned his confidence into new dread.

The first was a vine of silver on the trunk of the nearest tree. His eye had first mistaken it for dead ivy, but he saw now that it was a death-coil. One of Judy's death-coils. But why would she throw it at a tree? The second detail seemed to provide the beginnings of an answer. Caught in the fork of a branch that had fallen into the end of the depression, like a bit of grass itself, was a curl of reddish hair.

Michael guessed the situation in moments. Here Judy had encountered some creature—the owner of the bit of hair. She had thrown one coil and missed, but the second had hit its mark. But why, then, had Judy not come back to the ship? And where was the creature itself? Certainly, the creature might have been small enough for her to carry, and she could have gone back to the ship without his seeing her, but that seemed unlikely. He had after all seen no prints into the burn from the meadow. Suddenly noting more disturbances in the grass, Michael realized the other alternative. The creature had not been alone.

Pulling in his stomach, he stood up, raised the short-barrel and panned it along the trees, suddenly tense. Judy might have retreated from the meadow, but she had been gone long enough that something else was more likely: whatever had met her here had drawn or taken her away. Because the creature Judy had killed was also gone, Michael suspected that several more, still alive, must be involved. He realized, too, that since the creatures had taken their dead fellow, as well as Judy, with them, they must be intelligent. The thought made him back away toward the ship.

He should go back at once, he knew. Jeremy would know

what to do. Michael started backward, but he stopped before he reached the end of the grass. Time was a factor he had forgotten. If he took time to return to the ship and explain what had happened to Jeremy, Judy would be that much farther away. And Jeremy, Michael realized with a tingling in his stomach, would not be able to do more than Michael himself could do; one of them would have to stay with the ship, since there seemed to be intelligent creatures on this planet. Logic could give Jeremy that role; only he knew enough about the workings of the ship to defend it.

Michael suddenly realized that it was up to him to rescue Judy, or at least to follow her and find out something about her captors. And if he hoped to catch up with creatures more used to this terrain than he was, he should start right away. He could not even afford time to warn Jeremy; he would lose valuable moments explaining. His choice was chilling but clear cut. He started back toward the trees.

Even in the muddled shadows beneath the branches, he saw where the beings had left the meadow. The damp earth bore many impressions too garbled and faint to be read, and the prints stretched downhill through the trees, following a natural gap in the undergrowth. He set off with the short-barrel held up and his thumb on the activator button. Stark shadows striped across the trail, and faint flecks of light from the low sun scattered on his spacesuit and on the big leaves of the fern-trees. He felt no wind once the trees surrounded him, but he saw the highest branches twitching with its gusts.

The gap in the trees, which Michael had begun in his mind to call a trail, followed the edge of the hill but doubled back on itself, wending endlessly downward. At first he hardly noticed the slope, but soon the trees thinned away on one side to reveal a steep, tree-clad declivity ending in a valley flanked by two hills not quite as high as the one on which the rocket had landed. At the first break in the trees, he stopped and surveyed the landscape with his hand above his eyes. He saw only tree-covered hills, however, somber-looking rounded hills leading outward and downward, blotched with shadow and ruffled by the wind. He traced beyond them shapes of mountains. The sun was fast sinking toward an egg-shaped peak.

He noticed soon after leaving the hilltop that the forest was silent. No wind stirred the trees, and these below the top were of a different variety—most of them were thick and twisting, with flaccid, needle-thin leaves upon which drops from the last rain still collected. And the drip of branches around him, though considerable, made no sound, even when the drops met a silver pool in a hollow stump. His spacesuit had become hot and irritating, and his mouth had gone dry. But he did not dare drink Mirrorvaxan water.

He found the first clear prints in the mud alongside a rivulet at the bottom of the hill. The party seemed to have dispersed to cross the stream, so he found for the first time individual prints. A bootprint he thought at first to be Judy's, but when he found more, he looked at them all carefully. By this time the light was dim, however, so he could not decide whether the prints represented more than one pair of boots or not. If they did, that meant that the creatures were not only intelligent but also technologically advanced—to some extent. This thought both comforted and worried him. It also made him remember that they had Judy, and for all he knew, they may be planning to hurt her or even kill her. Blood rose in his cheeks when he thought of Judy being hurried along by tall, savage-looking creatures. He had often thought during training and even during the voyage that Judy might deserve such a fate. But something in the sinister silence of Mirrorvax had linked Judy to him; something made him forget her jeers and remember instead her bright, fierce eyes. He stopped himself short. He was worried about her, he muttered, because she, like him, was a part of Transvax, a very valuable and well-trained scientist. A part of Transvax that must be recovered.

He began to run, now following a ravine between the hills. Occasionally he glimpsed tracks in dying patches of sunlight, but he did not stop to look at them. In his suit and with the short-barrel, it was hard to run very fast, but he plodded on with scarcely a rest, hesitating only to leap a log or dodge a stump. Before long he was breathing so hard that he could not get enough air through the filter, so he ripped it off and threw it aside. He ran until running was all that he felt: the jar of his footfalls, the pound of his heart in his neck. He ran past landforms he hardly noticed, out of the ravine, across meadows, down more slopes, between closely pressing cliffs, through broad puddles, over hills, and into canyons. He noted only that he was still descending and that trees, now only silhouettes against the sky, were giving way to open country ahead, more level country, a river valley, perhaps. He could only just make it out in the thickening dusk. But whether Judy's captors were running or not, they kept ahead of him. He did not see them before the sun set.

His run ended abruptly on a brush-covered hillside, where his boot caught on a rock and sent him sprawling into the darkness. He took time getting up because the fall had knocked the breath from him, and his hand had scraped against the power-pack of the short-barrel. His palm felt damp, but it was too dark to see if his glove had ripped and if his hand was bleeding. And it was too dark, he noticed suddenly, putting the heel of his hand to his lips, to see anything but the pale-leaved bushes beside the trail. A few stars outlined mountains behind him and plains, marked by a few hills, ahead of him. But the Mirrorvaxan moon, no matter what it looked like, had not risen.

When he started along the trail once more, his leg caught on a bush and he tottered, nearly falling again. "Fool!" he said aloud, his voice losing itself in the vast wind-chilled blackness. He could not hope to find Judy in the dark. In fact, he was no longer sure he was still on her trail; his last sign of her, a temperature-monitoring instrument buried in the mud beside a stream, he had seen before the sun's rim touched the mountains. The thought

99

that in his headlong rush he had probably lost Judy, the ship, and himself as well made his mind sting. He cursed and propped the short-barrel against a rock. Then he put his head in his hands, pressing his scraped palm against his lips to keep from crying out.

The only thing he could do now, he realized, was wait for daylight or at least for the moon. Until that time he should rest. He lowered himself to the ground and leaned back against the rock, staring at the bright Mirrorvaxan stars in their strange constellations. He meant only to rest and not to sleep, and at first recurring stabs of dread and loneliness drove his drowsiness away. But the night lengthened, and no moon rose. Finally, the Mirrorvaxan night overcame him. He dropped into fitful sleep, his only comfort a length of cold Vaxan steel.

ANAMANDRA

HE EMERGED gradually from sleep, moving toward wakefulness in slow, imperceptible degrees. He first sensed light. Next he perceived dampness, moisture on his face and lips and in the earth-smelling air he breathed. Finally, as he realized his eyes were open, he felt pain: stiffness in his neck and thickness in his throat. Easing himself up on his elbows, he saw webbed branches of brush, their pale leaves jeweled with dew and dripping onto the reddish-brown earth and stone on which he had slept.

Groaning, he shook the water from his sleeves and then stood up. Mist hid the sky and smudged the hills around him so that he could make out little more than he had been able to the night before, even though the sun, a bright patch in the clouds, was already high. It was cold, too; cold enough that he shivered in spite of the insulation in his suit. And his throat, in spite of the dampness on his tongue, still felt dry. He winced whenever he swallowed.

He picked up the short-barrel, then rested it against his shoulder. "Filthy planet," he said aloud when he noticed mud on his pantlegs. He glared into the fog. The mist seemed to taunt him. It screened the landscape just enough to keep him from getting his bearings but not so much that he could justify waiting where he was.

He soon realized he had probably failed already. Judy was either beyond his reach or dead by now, and Jeremy back at the ship would be frenzied with worry and anger. Though Michael had done what he thought best by following Judy, Jeremy would still be furious. If, of course, Michael could find the ship again. He was not sure he could. He had come a long way, and Mirrorvax beneath fog looked very different from Mirrorvax in clear twilight. If he was lost—Michael shuddered at the sudden picture of the Director in his mind—that would be a blow to Transvax and to the mission. He could almost hear the Director's voice: "When you make mistakes or even miscalculations, Transvax pays for them. You don't. Even if you suffer because of your mistake, you don't pay—Transvax does. The important thing, then, is to repair the damage you have done to Transvax, no matter what discomfort you cause yourself. Repair it, I say. Turn any disadvantage into an advantage, each flaw into a strength, each miscalculation into an advance. If you do not, you have not served Transvax."

"Disadvantage into an advantage," Michael muttered. There seemed little chance of that. The best he could do would be to investigate the area a little more before he tried to find the ship. If he could find some sign of Judy or her captors, or even if he could discover a little more about Mirrorvax, his foray might not be totally in vain. If only Judy were somewhere near!

But the bushes marking the edge of his sight in the fog made him feel as if he were the planet's only inhabitant. The thought made him uneasy and prompted him to set off at a brisk pace along the trail. He moved off in the direction he had been going the night before, judging by his still-visible footprints, in hopes of finding some sign of Judy. But when he had crossed two brush-covered hills without seeing any other footprint in the damp earth, he realized Judy had not come this way. He had presumably turned off her path somewhere in the darkness the evening before. All he could do was backtrack in the hope of finding where he had gone wrong.

For some reason, however, he did not turn around right away. The idea of inching higher into the hills, peering at dew-smudged signs on the trail, did not appeal to him. He felt he needed some swift walking to warm himself up. And his throat ached so terribly now that he had to have a drink. Since the hills ahead seemed to be giving way to a broad, flat valley, he might find a river nearby. He could not remember how far away water was in the other direction.

Soon the path dropped from the last hill onto the flatland. The flat-topped brush, however, persisted, and since the shrub seemed better adapted to dry uplands than to river valleys, he suspected that no river might flow here, after all. So when he saw what looked like stumps off to his right, he left the trail and threaded his way among the bushes until he came to one.

But it was a chest-high length of log rather than a stump, and it, like others he could see spaced at intervals in either direction, seemed to be part-buried in the ground. More curious still, four metal wires (which he had at first mistaken for vines or lines of shadow) linked it with the posts farther off. This arrangement continued for as far as the fog would let him see.

The posts and wires were of course the product of some intelligent creature. But he had to stare at the thing for a long time before he could admit this to himself. Metal meant technology. And wire of this quality meant industry, at least on a primitive level. And industry meant the kind of civilization that would make it hard to rescue Judy and hard for Transvax to colonize this world, if the natives decided to resist. Forgetting for a moment the dryness in his mouth, he spat. This was an ugly twist of fate. He could not guess the purpose of the posts and wires, but he feared they formed a communication system. If so, what kind of messages might be buzzing along it, what word of the spaceship that had landed? What if, even now, orders were being sent for creatures of the planet to gather weapons around the *AOT* to destroy it?

He backed away from the post, heedless of the brush raking his boots, and raised the short-barrel. He pinched the activator button. The whine of the heat-packs smashed the silence of the fog. Then, steadying his eye on the nearest post, he squeezed the trigger.

A bolt of hot light licked out, meeting the post with a plume of red flame. But when the smoke drifted away into the fog and revealed a red gash where the post had been, Michael saw that the heat-contorted ends of the wires were not sparking. Perhaps, he thought, this system was low-voltage or not now being used. He extended the barrel of his weapon to let it cool. In any case, he had stopped the thing from being useful to the enemy.

Again unaccountably, he decided to follow the wires deeper into the flat. Thirst still goaded him, but curiously, it was mingled now with what Jeremy might have called fear; something told him he ought to learn more before returning to the ship. The warmth of the short-barrel comforted him as he moved along beside the wires. It was the only shred of Transvax power he had, and he was prepared to use it. He kept his finger on the activator switch and his eyes on the bushes ahead.

Perhaps because of the pain in his throat and the lingering odor of burning in his nose, he curled his lip at new smells coming in a freshening breeze. As if the spice-odor from the bushes weren't enough, he now smelled something even more pungent, something that reminded him of a waste-food processing plant. Maybe he was approaching a slow-running river. But the smell was not like algae, and the more odor he got, the more earthy it smelled, and the less he liked it. This planet was indeed filthy. Its mud caked on his boots and almost hobbled him; he had to stop at every other post to scrape them off. The inhabitants, even if they had technology, were foolish to leave their world in such a shabby state, so wild and wet. Their civilization must not be very great, even if they did have some technology, for it seemed they had not tamed their planet. But that would change, he thought, gripping the short-barrel. Yes, that would change. Transvax would make this world one worth visiting. They would mold splendors from this mud. Stooping to tighten his bootlaces, Michael vowed that he would do everything he could—fly the AOT back to Vax by himself if he had to—to make that dream come true.

He walked for quite a distance, but nothing in the landscape changed. Then just when he was ready to start back to the ship, the terrain did seem different. The brush suddenly gave way to an open stretch of red-brown earth, ridged as if a huge comb had been drawn across it. This open space yielded to tall, pale-green plants, rushes perhaps, on its far end. On the other side of the wires the brush continued.

This clearing, too, had been made by intelligent creatures. But again he could not guess its use, for it was not solid enough to be a landing pad and it seemed too isolated and empty to be used for agriculture. But it was nonetheless a sign that he was nearing a concentration of native settlement; it was a cue for him to take care. If the creatures had surprised Judy, they could surprise him, and the rushes were tall enough to hide them. He wished, suddenly, that he had brought death-cords along. For he could not activate the short-barrel without firing it, and he did not want to reveal his position any more clearly that he had done already, in case some of the creatures were stalking him. Yet considering the moments the short-barrel would take to activate made him nervous.

He kept deep in the open as he crossed the clearing. He did not know what kind of weapons the enemy had, but it would be foolish to keep to the underbrush, where an ambush might surprise him. At least in the open he could see.

Halfway to the rushes he saw that the wires ended at a

final post. Maybe the lines went underground. And well they might, for through gaps in the rushes, he saw that a river ran perpendicular to the clearing. It was, from the look of it, a slow river; dark water foamed with mist. But even so the movement of the water, audible when he reached a hard-packed length of earth paralleling its bank, turned his thirst to madness. Forgetting caution, he broke into a run. He reached the rushes, burst through them to the brink of the flow, and then, heedless of the mud or the condition of the water, he propped the short barrel against his knee, knelt, and scooped cool water to his lips. He gulped it hungrily enough that he scarcely noticed its taste until he had washed the dryness, though not the rawness, away. Then he glanced toward the opposite bank, which rose amid mist-woven reeds, before he bent to drink again.

But he had hardly dipped his hand into the water a second time when he heard a voice. It rippled across the surface of the water, speaking in odd syllables that registered in the translator still in his ear:

"You shouldn't drink that water. The cows have been in it!"

He bolted to his feet. But in so doing, he knocked the short-barrel with his knee, and it toppled to splash into the shallows. He snatched for it, but when he saw the current tugging the end of the heat pack into the water, he spun around and with a terrific leap sprang through the rushes and flattened himself face-down against the earth.

Lightning dogged his heels. A sound like screaming thunder shot over him, followed by a bolt of searing heat, which flashed across the legs of his suit. A roar of fire followed, and in its wake came snapping flames and heat-driven smoke that scattered over the empty field. Then a second rush of heat poured over him, bearing with it steam and crisped remnants of water reeds. Then came more smoke, thick and acid-smelling, fibrous smoke that engulfed and smothered him. Long before it thinned, he was coughing, then choking, then writhing for air. At last his mind swam into near-unconsciousness; bitter blackness made him go limp.

The next thing he knew, something was grasping his arm and turning him over onto his back. He found himself coughing violently but drawing in gusty breaths of fresh air. Unless it was a hallucination, a voice in the translator earphone pierced the darkness and the ringing in his head. "By the Canons, are you all right? What *was* that? Hey, are you all right?"

His mind brinked again on unconsciousness, and a tentacled vision of the thing that might be speaking swam through his mind. He moaned and tried to raise his arm, but it swayed, and if something had not caught it, it would have fallen. The something—he was quite helpless to prevent it—worked off his glove and closed around his wrist. What grasped him had the feel of a human hand, just as the voice had seemed high-pitched but human. But that, he knew, was probably only because he was familiar with nothing else.

"What are you?" he asked groggily. "Who are you?"

"You're mumbling," the voice hummed in his ear. The grip placed his hand on his chest. Something touched his cheek a moment later. "I can't understand a word you're saying. Are you hurt?"

At least the thing seemed to want to help him. But that was probably deceptive. In either case, he was at its mercy. If it was going to kill him, he wished it would do so quickly, before he had recovered enough to feel it. Tasting smoke still, he cursed himself for his carelessness with the short-barrel and the Transvax scientists for not inventing a reciprocal element for the translating device.

"At least you're breathing," the voice went on, "and at least your pulse is strong. Fast, yes; but mine is, too. I was sitting on the bridge down the road when I heard you go through the rushes and start to drink. I'm sorry I startled you—but the cows pasture down here, and my mother always says not to drink canal water. But then I saw you dive away, and suddenly the whole canal lit up like lightning, and steamed as if all the water in it were being boiled up. I thought you would be—" The voice stopped itself. Fingers rested on his cheek. Then the voice went on, slowing down, "I would have died of fright myself if it hadn't been as far away from me as it was. But you—how badly are you hurt? Did you get burned?"

He forced open his eyes, but for moments he saw only blackness. His eyes, as they cleared, focused first on the charred ridge of earth and the stubble of reeds that marked the place he had knelt to drink. Vapor still rose from the canal, and a few reeds were burning on its far bank. Smoke still drifted over him, but some of it was blocked by the being he had heard speak, who rose to its knees and withdrew its hands when he opened his eyes.

He found himself staring at a girl.

He knew it was a girl even though she wore a pale-green garment, something like a robe but closer-fitting and embroidered on its sleeves with green and white leaves and flowers. A bit of cloth, the same material as the robe, bound part of her hair, which fell past her shoulders and was the color of strained honey. Her eyes, however, were charcoal-black and glistening, something like wide dark mirrors; and when they touched his, he stiffened.

The being, except for the color of her hair and eyes, might have passed as a Vaxan; indeed, because of her long hair, she reminded him of the girl he had met in the auction complex at Medracar. Her expression, too, was human; her lips parted in curiosity, and her eyes registered surprise, probably at the color of his own.

"Are you . . . are you all right?" she asked, drawing back.

"No," he said, lifting himself a little.

His voice seemed to startle her. Whether what he had just said meant anything to her or not he could not guess, nor did he want to know. He had prepared himself for anything on Mirrorvax but this; he would have preferred the creature to be subhuman or grotesque. Something inside him cried out that it was horrible for her to be so human, so Vaxan, when he knew that beneath her pale skin was something alien and uncanny. Despite a new fit of dizziness, he lifted himself up with his arms and began to edge away. She opened her mouth as if to speak, but she said nothing. As soon as he was out of her reach, he staggered to his feet and began to back away.

But seeing her motionless on the fire-blackened ground, flanked on one side by the steaming canal and the smoldering rushes and on the other by what he now guessed to be a road, leading upriver toward a plank bridge on the edge of the fog, he hesitated. To run seemed the most sensible thing to do. But, feeling smoke tingling still in his lungs and seeing the blackened patches on his sleeves, he wondered how far he could get. If this girl raised the alarm and brought others, whether she knew he was an outworlder or not, he would have little chance for escape and would end up little better than Judy. If he was careful, on the other hand, he might be able to use the girl to his advantage. As long as she did not suspect him for what he was, he might be able to get valuable information from her, possibly news of where others of her kind had taken Judy.

Panting, he backed up against one of the posts and leaned against it. Giddiness swept over him, and it was only by gripping the wires that he kept his feet. Seeing his weakness, the girl stood up and moved toward him. But he frowned at her until she stopped.

"You *are* hurt," she said. He followed her eyes to a gash in his suit at his knee, where he had probably scraped a rock throwing himself to the ground. "Why won't you let me help you? I won't hurt you!"

This time Michael took note of her true speech as well as the translation. Her language had a tonal quality not unlike his own, and he could almost discern elements of it. She started toward him again; eyebrows lowered, hands outstretched. He shook his head violently.

"No?" she said, stopping again.

109

He noted the word in her language, then repeated it emphatically. "No."

"No? Why not? Why won't you let me help you?"

"No," he said again. He had to increase his vocabulary quickly, or he had no chance of allaying her suspicions. That she might guess who he was seemed unlikely. She seemed far more primitive than he. And she seemed young. But he could not take any chances. His mind had begun to buzz now, and the wire pressed into his hands where he was gripping it. "No," he said breathlessly.

"You're hurt," she said, her voice sharper. She edged nearer, "And I think you don't know how badly hurt you are. Believe me, I won't hurt you. How could I hurt you? I only want to help you. That's all. You should let me, for your own good. I don't know what happened by the canal, but you were nearer to it than I was—"

The girl was interrupted by shouts out of the fog, and then the pounding of feet on the bridge. Turning his head, Michael saw that two boys had crossed the canal and were running toward the girl. Something told him to run, but he knew if he let go of the wires, he would fall.

"Anamandra! Anamandra!" The translator did not change the word they shouted, but it was only after the boys reached the girl and, suddenly noticing Michael, took a stance on either side of her, that Michael realized the word was probably the girl's name. That the girl would have a name and acquaintance with at least two others made his mind buckle again.

"Anamandra," the shorter boy said, taking her arm, "what was that noise? We heard it even at the house. Mother told us you had come this way this morning. She sent us to see if you were all right."

The girl kept her eyes on Michael. "I am all right."

"And who is that?" the taller boy said, lifting an arm toward Michael. Both boys wore pale-blue outfits, something like the uniforms Michael had worn at the Flats but sleeveless. The tall one's shoulders tightened under his shirt when he noticed Michael's spacesuit and the burned patches on it. "Ana," he whispered, "who is he?"

"I don't know, Corbi," the girl said. "But he's hurt. Run back to the house, will you? See if father is home from Snowhold yet—"

"He isn't," the tall boy said, shaking a head sprouting with red-orange hair. "Aric and I were just there a few minutes ago. And you know he said he might not be back home for a week—"

"Tell Mother to come, then," the girl said. She pushed against the boy's back. "Go!"

The tall boy began to run, but Michael knew suddenly that he could not afford to have news about him spread. In a surge of desperation, he cried out, "No!" The boy stopped short.

The girl opened her mouth, as if to urge him to go on. Loosening his grip on the wires, Michael sank to his knees, then to his haunches. Then he managed to blurt out, reddening with anger and pain, "No, Anamandra." Mention of her name made her grip the other boy's arm. And her eyes went wide when he almost whispered the one word he had gleaned from her: "Help."

"Corbi," Anamandra snapped to the red-headed boy, "come back." She looked at both of them, then at Michael. "I want you two to help me bring this man to the house. He is hurt—"

"Who is he?" demanded the shorter boy, still at Anamandra's side. "How did he get here? Where is he from? What happened to him? Ana, you don't know this man, do you? He's a stranger. He looks foreign. Mother will be upset if you bring a stranger to the house. You know what she says about strangers—"

"I also know what the Canons say about strangers," the girl said, moving closer to Michael. She motioned for each of the boys to take one of Michael's arms. The boys seemed as wary of him as he was of them; but with urging from Anamandra, they took hold of him gingerly and propped him up. Michael tolerated them and stood between them only because there was nothing else he could do. His last thought of resistance died with a further rise of weakness in his body. He was helpless now—his short-barrel had nearly killed him, and the few words he knew in the Mirrorvaxan language had only committed him to a captivity like Judy's. They would certainly kill him when they found out who he was, but perhaps he could forestall that. This last flicker of hope seemed false, but he clung to it. If he could play along with them long enough to regain his strength, he might have a chance for escape.

He tottered along between the boys, hating the feel of their grip, cringing at Anamandra's voice beside him. As the plank-bridge grew nearer, and as he began to glimpse more posts and wires on the far side of the canal in the fog, Michael bowed his head in despair. To be captured at all was the final result of his foolishness; but to be caught by a young native girl and her even younger brothers, all of them at an age where they would probably still be resource on Vax, harrowed him. Still, it pained him far more that he had failed, that even with artillery and with the finest training Transvax had given him, he had been subdued by a few feckless members of a primitive society. And perhaps, he thought when they reached the bridge, fate would give him no chance to redeem himself for Transvax.

THE BROTHER
OF DEATH

"WE STILL DON'T KNOW who this man is or where he comes from," the boy Anamandra had called Aric said as they approached the bridge. His hair, the same color as Anamandra's but more roughly cropped, half-hid the same kind of mirror-black eyes. "We don't even know his name."

"We don't," Anamandra said, "but do we need to? Remember, we don't know *His* name. And shouldn't we be able to help someone without knowing anything about him? Isn't that what the Thirteenth Canon says?"

"I didn't know you had read the Canons," Corbi said. He grunted as Michael's weight shifted to him. You seem pretty righteous all of a sudden."

"Yes, with us doing all the work," Aric said. "He's heavy, you know."

"You still haven't told us what that noise was," Corbi said.

"That's because I don't know," Anamandra said, pausing at the bridge to look back. "He may know, but I don't think he can tell us yet. He's hurt, badly hurt. He may be in shock." Michael kept his eyes down; the girl, at least, believed that his silence was due to the explosion of the short-barrel. He must let them believe he was indeed in shock.

It would not be a hard part to act. And if it could buy him time, time to piece together the language and regain his strength, it would be worth the effort. Above all he needed strength.

The boys helped him onto the bridge, but his boot caught on the plank and he pitched forward. The dark canal loomed as he fought to regain his balance. Aric grunted, and Corbi squeaked, "Oh, Anamandra! Come here! Help us get him across the bridge, at least!"

She dropped back and replaced Aric. With all three of them holding him, they brought him to the packed earth and the pair of ruts on the far side of the canal. When Anamandra surrendered her post to Aric, she was still breathing hard, and her hair seemed wind-rumpled.

"Now you can quote the Canons all you want," Corbi said.

Before they had gone far on the road, the fog began to thin and Michael could see that the place was indeed a broad river valley. It continued far, flat and almost featureless, until it ended in gray-green hills, presumably brush-covered uplands like the ones where he had spent the night. By the lines of rushes and horizons of sparse trees, he guessed canals patterned much of the valley floor. Posts followed the ruts of the road on one side, and Michael at last realized that the stump-and-wire arrangement served the same purpose as concrete walls and aluminum fences did on Vax—but much less efficiently, for the same tall grass that filled the strip between the ruts spilled from the side of the road, under the wires and far into the flatland, which he presumed ought to be cleared like the field he had seen earlier. What was more, beneath some distant trees, half a dozen beasts clumped, some of them grazing, some of them lying down. The wretched cows the girl had mentioned, no doubt. This world's techniques of agriculture seemed primitive indeed, for even their fences could not keep the cows from their fields or away from their canals. When the breeze brought the odor of the cows to him, he winced. They were what he had smelled before; if only he had been wise enough to start back to the ship then.

More smells came, most of them sour. The fog lifted enough that Michael could see the road curving toward a cluster of low buildings sheltered by a line of wind-curved trees. A mud-colored plank building he guessed to be a primitive stable or storage barn. A small building, in even worse repair, probably held seed or housed small animals. The third building was half-hidden by trees and by the barn, but he saw that it was taller than the others. It had probably once been painted white, but now it was streaked with gray. Tiles on its roof were missing, and the one upper window he could see glared at him, small and beady.

These people were indeed primitive, he thought. Why, they were scarcely better than savages if their settlement amounted to no more than this. If he still had the short-barrel, he could level all three of the buildings with a few shots. Even if there were many more of these settlements, a Transvax team with artillery could liquidate them all within a few weeks. And the inhabitants would obviously benefit from Transvax's takeover. They were clearly ignorant, untidy, and possibly barbaric. But certainly they must have the modicum of intelligence necessary to learn trades from Transvax teachers. These very boys could in time be made bricklayers or woodcutters for the new Vaxan colony.

"Mother won't let you bring him in," Corbi said to Anamandra, "not while Father is away. No matter what the Canons say."

By this time Michael was growing weary of their prattle about things he did not understand. They obviously lived in a primitive family group, which meant that their parents were probably as ignorant as they were. He stomached a spasm of pain. If only he could escape—with what he knew so far, he could fill up a dozen voice-tapes. If he could once reach the ship, he would already have enough information for a colonization recommendation to the Transvax tribunal.

"What else can Mother do?" Anamandra said. "Leave him out to die?"

"For heaven's sake, Anamandra. He isn't going to die."

"But he looks terrible." Her eyes touched him. "Look how red his face is. Don't you see the burns on his clothes? He probably can't even hear us."

"Whatever Mother will do, we're almost home," Aric said. "Look. Here comes Elissa!"

Elissa, apparently, meant the girl who had appeared down the road and was running toward them, a waist-high animal galloping at her side. The girl, just taller than Corbi, had the same color hair he did and wore a pale-yellow outfit that seemed a smaller version of Anamandra's. Michael noticed her less than he did her wolfish companion, a brute with a silly expression and a frowsy coat. The creature reached him long before the girl did and began sniffing at him, barking and frisking almost beneath his feet until one of the boys aimed a kick at it. Michael had seen a similar Vaxan animal, as part of his resource training. But it had been behind glass or stuffed (he couldn't remember which), and the beast that now met him was so active and smelly that he had to clench his teeth to preserve his pretense of half-consciousness. This sort of beast Vaxan colonists would not find useful and would fortunately eliminate. The thought came to him that if the colonists had orders similar to his own, even the natives would have to be eliminated —at least the ones who resisted the new order of things. When he remembered that his own instructions had been to kill any possibly dangerous life-forms on sight, a wave of weakness dragged over him. It was only when he remembered he was a captive and that these beings, no matter how harmless they seemed, might mean his death, that at last he saw the logic of what the trainers had tried to teach him.

116

Still, he was somehow relieved he did not have the short-barrel.

The second girl stopped short, a few paces away. "By the Canons," she squealed, "where did you find *him?*" She began backing up in pace with them, staring at Michael. He noticed she had brownish spots—dirt probably—all over her cheeks.

"We didn't *find* him," Anamandra retorted, narrowing her eyes. "It isn't as if we simply picked him up off the ground. I *met* him down by the canal bridge. But there was an explosion of some kind. He was near it. He's hurt."

"Are you sure he's safe?" Elissa asked. Catching the wolfish animal's collar, she sized Michael with her eyes. "He's pretty big."

"As if we didn't know," Corbi said, kicking at a dirt clod. "How much farther do we have to go, El? I can't see. Sweat is getting in my eyes."

"You're almost to the barn," Elissa said.

"Thank goodness for that," Anamandra said. "Elissa, go fetch Mother, will you?"

"I don't have to," Elissa replied. "She's already on the porch. We've been watching you come almost since you came to this side of the south pasture."

When Michael lifted his eyes, he saw that they had indeed passed the first of the buildings. It sank behind before he could get a look at it. He found himself then in a dirt-floored yard, roughly triangular, where another beast, smaller and black but of the same species as the first, dashed through a congregation of noisy birds, scattering them, to reach Elissa and Anamandra. A few more animals peered from a slat fence in front of a small shed, and birds flooded out of one of the many trees growing haphazardly around the yard. A few of them circled and roosted on the crest of the third building, toward which all of them moved.

This, Michael presumed, was the house. But he could not imagine even these savages living in it. Its peaked roof

117

cramped its second floor, and the windows of its lower story were obscured by bushy trees in a lawn in front of it. The trees had showered a chaos of twigs and leaves over the plank walk to the door and on the crooked roof over the entry-way. Posts that propped this roof had, like the planks of the house walls, once been white; but now they were gray, notched and streaked with weather.

A woman stood between them, on stone steps that led to the door.

She was short, rather stout, and slightly bent; the skin of her face and her hands, cradling something wrapped in a blanket, was sunburned and weathered. Her complexion and her size made her seem to be of a different Mirror-vaxan race from her children, though she wore the same fashion of clothing. Her eyes, however, were as black and fathomless as Anamandra's. She fixed them on Michael as he approached. He could not bear to look at her. He hung his head and watched the boards of the walk pass until the first stone step came into view.

"Anamandra," he heard a soft, resonant voice say from the porch. "Who is this?"

"I don't know his name," Anamandra said, "and I don't know where he comes from. I found him—I *met* him, I mean—down by the canal. He has been hurt—"

"By the same thing that made the noise we heard," Corbi put in.

Out of the corner of his eye, Michael saw the woman studying him. "Sir," the woman said stiffly, "what business do you have on our farm? What are you doing in Rush Valley?"

"What do you mean, what is he doing?" Anamandra protested.

"Softly, Ana, or you will wake the baby," Elissa whispered.

"He is not from the valley," the woman said, "and by the look of him, not from the Near Valleys."

Michael clenched his teeth; the woman, unfortunately,

knew at least something more than her children. But surely she did not suspect— "He *does* look foreign," Anamandra said, "but does that matter? He is a man, isn't he. He is one of His children, isn't he? The Thirteenth Canon says—"

"I know what the Canons say, Anamandra," the woman interrupted her. Her voice, because of its evenness, disconcerted Michael. "Sir," she said, addressing him again, "my name is Katandra Amudsar, and because you do indeed seem hurt, I would like to help you. But I must know more about you before I can—"

"He won't answer, Mother," Anamandra broke in. "He can't. He's in shock. You can see that. You weren't by the canal when the thunder happened. I was. From what I saw, this man is lucky to be alive. We have to help him."

The woman opened her mouth, but she glanced at Michael and then closed her lips. She nodded, very slowly. "Hold the baby," she told Elissa, who took the form in the blanket and moved to the side of the porch. Anamandra and her mother stared at one another while the boys struggled to bring Michael up the steps and through a dim doorway.

They brought him into a small room duskily lit by a curtained window. "Put him on the couch," Anamandra's mother said. While the two boys helped him to a dusty, cloth-covered sofa, she lit a lamp and set it on a ledge above a fireplace. Faint light scattered over the room, revealing a worn carpet of indiscernible colors and two threadbare chairs set to face the couch. Corbi and Aric helped Michael rest back against an arm of the couch, until his head touched a cushion Anamandra brought for him. The room smelled of ashes and of something musty, but other smells came from a better-lit room through a doorway, where Michael glimpsed a wooden table. Aric stooped to unlace his boots, but he seemed puzzled by their latchings. After a nod from his mother, he lifted Michael's legs onto the couch.

"Now out, all of you," Katandra Amudsar said. "Elissa,

see if you can put the baby to sleep."

"But we want to stay," Corbi said. Aric echoed him with a nod.

"Feed the dogs and the chickens while you're at it," she said. "Out, I say. If this man is in shock, he hardly needs all of you staring at him." The boys frowned, but Aric led Corbi out the front door, and Elissa drifted into the next room, swinging the baby rhythmically in her arms.

"May I stay, Mother?" Anamandra asked. She had pulled one of the chairs nearer the sofa, and now she sat on the edge of it, leaning toward Michael. He kept his eyes half-closed and pretended not to notice her.

"Stay, by all means. I will have questions to ask you, once we have seen to this man." She moved beside Michael and bent over him. He let his eyes fall closed so he would not have to endure her eyes. He knew she must be examining his face. She touched his cheek and forehead with cool fingers, then put her hand to his throat, just below his jaw. She parted a tear in the leg of his spacesuit, repeated her first procedure, then said to Anamandra, "He doesn't seem badly hurt. But he may be in shock. And he may have a fever. Bring a cloth and a water pail from the kitchen." Michael cracked his eyes to watch Anamandra hurry to the other room, where she placed a tin bucket beneath a faucet, pumped a handle half a dozen times, then returned, off-balanced by the pail. She placed it by the side of the couch, dipped a cloth into it, and handed it to her mother. "You can care for him as well as I can," Katandra Amudsar said. "I have work enough to do without having to care for the strangers you bring home. He needs very little attention, Ana. What he needs most is rest. And time to regain his senses. Sponge his face, if it feels hot, and bring a blanket if he shivers. He should need little more for the time being." She started toward the kitchen. "If he seems worse, Anamandra, call me. I won't be far away."

In spite of apprehension and pain, Michael had begun to feel drowsy. But when Anamandra began dabbing at his cheeks with a cold cloth, he opened his eyes almost involuntarily. She drew the cloth away, hesitated, then smiled. "It will help bring your fever down," she explained. She immersed the cloth, wrung it out, and applied it cautiously to his temples. He glared as her as she gingerly pushed the hair back from his forehead. If he indeed had a fever, this would do very little good; it infuriated him to have to subject himself to such primitive treatment. But for the time being, he seemed to have no choice.

She pretended not to see his scowl and continued to bathe his forehead. Eventually she said, as if to herself, "Mother thinks you are foreign."

He let his eyes drift closed again. The cold cloth touched his temples. He wished he could be almost anywhere but under Anamandra's black-eyed stare. He felt naked, somehow; and he could not remove hot anger from his cheeks. If only he had turned back before coming to the canal. If only he had the strength now to run, to escape the settlement and return to the ship.

"I *would* like to know your name," she said, still working the cloth. "That is, if you don't mind."

The girl requested this, he was sure, so she would have more information to bear to her mother later. He resolved to stay on guard. But reconsidering, he thought there would be little harm in telling her that much. His language would mean nothing to her, and if she already thought he was foreign, it might lead her to accept him as someone from another part of her own world. He opened his eyes.

"Will you tell me?" she persisted.

"Michael," he said. "Michael 2112—"

"Maicyl Tuwin?" she interrupted with a sudden smile. "Maicyl Tuwin? That is an odd name, but a nice one." The intonation of his natural language seemed to have convinced her he was foreign, because she said, "You can't understand our language very well, can you?"

This was a dangerous question to answer, but because she was looking at him, he answered in her language, "No."

"Then it isn't any wonder you have been confused," she said, more to herself than to him. Putting the cloth aside, she said in a slow, deliberate voice, "How—much—do—you—understand, Maicyl?"

He wished he could tell her he understood every word she said. Again he cursed the Transvax scientists for not finishing their invention. But since this seemed a good chance to pick up more of the language, he lifted his hand and pinched his forefinger and thumb toward one another until they met.

"I see," she said. The glitter in her eyes made him uneasy. "Maybe I can teach you more of it, if you feel well enough—"

"Anamandra," her mother's voice came from the kitchen. "Come here, please."

With a final smile at Michael, she stood up and disappeared into the kitchen. Michael swallowed painfully; she would take everything she had just learned from him to her mother. He heard her repeating his name, even now. He wished he had said nothing. He lifted his head and tried to push himself up with his elbows, but his head began to swim, and he relaxed again. Blackness edged in, and the barking he heard from outside and the crying from somewhere above seemed suddenly dreamlike. Anamandra's voice brought him back to full consciousness. She stood above him, holding a steaming mug in both hands. "Broth," she said, sitting down beside him. "This is broth."

"Broth," he croaked. This was hardly the kind of vocabulary he needed.

She leaned over him. "Drink," she said. She propped his head with her hand and brought the container close to his lips. The steam from it was nothing like Michael had ever smelled. It tingled pleasantly in his nose and awakened fierce hunger in his stomach. Still, he could not think of drinking something hot, as this obviously was. What kind of barbarians were these people? He would be wise to expect poison in this "broth," since the mother of the family knew more about him than she admitted to her children. And even if she had not poisoned it intentionally, his system must certainly react badly to Mirrorvaxan food. Besides, how could he tell if its preparation had been at all sanitary? This planet was primitive, and those people seemed to have no regard for cleanliness. After all, if they kept smelly animals in their barns and loose in their yard . . .

"Drink," Anamandra said again. It was no longer vocabulary. "Mother says you will need strength. This will give it to you."

Strength, Michael thought. Sniffing at the steam again, he decided to take the chance. He allowed Anamandra to bring the cup to his lips. He took a sip. The taste was shocking. It was not pleasantly bland, like the Syntac nutritional preparations he was used to. It was salty and warm and rich in a kind of flavor he was not sure he liked. After a few more draughts, he motioned for her to take it away. She did so, but he was almost sorry. The broth eased his hunger and did make him feel stronger. But the pain in his throat made it hard to swallow.

"Good," Anamandra said when she returned. "Do you feel better? Yes?"

"Yes," he said. She felt his forehead, then brought out the pail again. "Cloth," she said, showing it to him. "Cold cloth."

The mere notion of being patronized by an outworld savage, so obviously his inferior, made Michael set his jaw. But remembering his need to learn this language and to keep these people from becoming suspicious, he repeated, through set teeth, "Cold cloth."

Anamandra beamed. She laid a finger and said. "Fever." When he had echoed her, she said. "Cold cloth for fever."

He mimmicked her, taking careful note of the pitch of her voice. Her language was not terribly different from his own. He wondered if she knew that she had taught him several nouns, an adjective, and a preposition. He doubted if she did. Probably speaking her language was almost instinct to her. A society like this would never bother to educate its inhabitants. It would be a much more pleasant place when Transvax had organized it. Perhaps some of the more intelligent natives could be trained as interpreters, so none of the colonists would have to learn the language if they wanted servants. Vaxan would probably be too complex for these primitive people to learn. And if some of them were hostile, as Judy's captors had been, the Transvax Secretariat might order the native population to be strictly controlled.

Anamandra persisted in naming things for him: the couch, parts of her face, the furnishings of the room, the trees outside of the window. Though sometimes she would correct his pronunciation, when she pointed to things and had Michael name them, she raised her eyebrows when he got all of them correct. She couldn't know, of course, that having been trained as an advocate, he had memorized far more difficult lists than the words of her simple language. But if a simple act like that amazed her, so much the better: she would be more amazed when she saw the real power of his world. He folded his arms across his chest and smiled.

But she only smiled back and began to teach him more words, some for objects and some for more abstract ideas that he would surely have misunderstood from her gestures if he had not had the translator. Finally though, he began to grow weary under the strain of assimilation, and soon he grew confused listening to the translator in one ear and her language in the other. He repeated phrases in his own language. When he did this, Anamandra laughed, said, "Maicyl, no," and repeated the words again. At first he laughed back, because her language sounded as peculiar to him as his might to her. But he grew increasingly confused and growingly abashed by her laughter. Finally, when his ears began to buzz and his throat to throb, he stopped speaking.

Anamandra at first tried to make him go on, but he

sealed his lips. Pain, before only vague, had begun to sharpen all through his body. But particularly it gripped his throat, which now felt so inflamed he could scarcely breath through it. He moaned and turned his head away from her.

Her hand flew to his forehead. Her flesh was chill against his. At once she immersed the cloth again and began to stroke his forehead and cheeks. She spoke softly to him, some kind of apology for straining him, but he did not bother to listen. Fuzzy images reared up in his mind. Odd sounds bawled in his ears, sounds like artillery warming up, noises of hatches closing, sounds of voices, one of them the Director's. He felt the cloth on his face only vaguely. It did not any longer tighten his skin or invite him to alertness. He felt cold, though, and he imagined his fingernails were really ice and that Anamandra had soaked a blanket with ice water before laying it on him. Some time later he tried to lift his head, but hands helped it down again, cold hands, hands made of snow that pushed back his hair and pressed against his forehead.

"His fever is much worse, Anamandra," a voice said. "Much worse. You should have come for me the moment he stopped talking."

"I looked for you," another voice said, sounding broken. "Elissa said you had gone to the road to meet someone. I ran all the way to the gate!" Michael's mind reeled. He had somehow lost track of time, perhaps several hours. Blackness was closing in again, this time even thicker—but warm with odd, reddish sparks that crackled as the darkness advanced. "I am worried about him, Mother," Anamandra's voice continued. "Look how pale he is. He's shivering, even under all those blankets. I had Elissa stay with him when I went for you. She said he was crying out things she couldn't understand. Mother, what is it? Fever?"

"More than fever. Anamandra, this is very serious. There is only one thing we can do. Have you caught your breath enough to run? Good. Then hurry to Wolscots and bring Brother Wolscot and Imrand back with you."

"Fever," Michael muttered in his own language, "fever." But it was indeed more than fever. In a flash of clear-mindedness, he realized what was wrong. It had nothing to do with the explosion of the short-barrel; he had come away from that almost unscathed. And it probably had little to do with the broth he had taken. It had begun, he realized, when he had taken off his filter on the mountain trail. In all the excitement, he had forgotten about bacteria. He heard Judy laughing at him for forgetting. But it was a dead laugh. Judy herself might be dead, and Michael soon would be. Bacteria swelled his throat. They riddled his system, countless by now; countless, alien, and deadly. In the care of savages, he had no hope for survival. Even Vaxan technology would be hard-pressed to save his life. Here, in the hands of these ignorant natives, there seemed little chance that he would outlive a contest with the planet's microorganisms. He tried to shout out to Anamandra that she must see that he got back to the ship, but his words were garbled, and she would not understand his language even if he could speak clearly.

He heard Katandra Amudsar's voice speaking to him softly. But her words blurred and became the utterance of an auction complex computer, sounding again and again, showing the digit o repeatedly on a screen. "Recyclage!" a voice in his mind snarled. "Recyclage and broth!" His mind cloaked itself with darkness, lit up with threads of pain like lightning in a night sky. Flocks of noisy airships swarmed across his mind, each bearing a piece of him, each lit up by bolts of pain. They faded away to be replaced by flashes of planets and trees and uniforms and complexes. Then they yielded to pictures too swift and dim for Michael to identify.

After an indeterminate time he heard footfalls and breathing, and the rustle of fabric and voices. One voice was Anamandra's mother, who brought two other voices, a deep one and a tenor one, toward him in the darkness. The translator in his ear brought snatches of their talk to him, but he understood it only slightly. The floor creaked. The low voice boomed very near him. He turned his head to the side and felt dampness between it and his pillows. A hand touched his face. A second pair of hands, heavy and rough, rested on his head, and a lighter pair rested beside them. Dizziness spun his mind until he thought the hands were birds roosting in his hair.

But then the voice, above the crackle of feverish darkness, began to speak. Its tune was slow and even, and he heard each word as if it were the only one the man had spoken. But oddly, the microphone in his ear provided no translation. Perhaps it had gone dead. Perhaps he himself was dead and listening to the voice of the cosmos speaking in the void.

The voice fell silent, and the hands lifted. Michael's eyelids fluttered. He caught sight of two men turning toward Katandra Amudsar and of darkness beyond the door of the house. He closed his eyes and turned to his side. One of his hands went to his throat and followed its smoothness down from his chin, trying to find the lumps of pain he knew were there. They were there—they had to be. But he was far too tired to find them. The voices continued, some distance away. He heard Anamandra talking about drinking from the canal.

Then, like dark, misty water, sleep swept over him.

MORNING

HE AWOKE when butterflies of light from the window above the couch struck his eyes. They sported on his face, skimmed across his blankets, and flocked on the worn carpet, pale and glittering. They moved with a kind of sighing music, and when Michael sat up and peered through the curtains, he saw why. Morning light fell through the branches of the trees, and the sun, breaking over the hills, seemed about to climb a steel-blue sky.

"Maicyl," a soft voice said. He turned to see that a triangle of light from the opening he had made in the curtains fell on Anamandra. She sat, hands on her knees, in the same chair she had used the evening before. Or had it been the morning before? Assuming that he should still be sick or at least dizzy, Michael lay down again. She smiled at him and asked, "How do you feel, Maicyl?"

He sighed, then said, "Good." Dazed, he thought, would have described his state better, but his Mirrorvaxan vocabulary was still unelaborate. And, strangely enough, he did feel good; better, at least, then he had felt the day before. His throat no longer hurt, and his head was clear, and he felt no pain except perhaps the sun in his eyes.

Anamandra stood up. "I'll bring you some breakfast,"

she said. He noticed, though it scarcely seemed important, that she wore new clothing, a dress something like the one she had worn before, but gold in color and trimmed with lace. Yet the dress was not Medron-gold but instead pale-gold, something near the color of Anamandra's hair, which now, unbound, rested on her shoulders. She backed toward the kitchen but kept her eyes on him, so she nearly collided with Elissa, who appeared in the doorway.

"Watch where you're going," Elissa said. Then she added, "Or are you watching something better?" She eyed Anamandra's dress. "Or are *both* of you watching something better?"

"You'll have to forgive Elissa," Anamandra said loftily. "She's *very* young." Elissa giggled, but Anamandra pushed her into the kitchen, where their voices lost themselves in the clank of crockery. Michael had understood very little of the whole exchange, so he hardly felt able to forgive Elissa, whatever she had done. And he did not care about their petty doings. His mind was clear now, and his purpose was firm. He would escape the first moment possible. Now that he was no longer sick—

He stopped himself. He knew he had been sick. Very sick. Sickness was not something that happened often on the ordered world of Vax, but he had had a throat disease once as a child and had studied illnesses enough to know that he had just weathered a serious one. One that might have killed him, in fact: the Space Corporation scientists had said that any bacteria they might encounter here would be deadly, because as out-worlders they would have no natural resistance to it. If they were infected, the scientists had told them, even Vaxan technology would be hard-pressed to save them. Michael had forgotten this and had taken off his filter. He had become infected. Then why was he still alive, and why, further, had all the symptoms of the infection vanished?

He explored his throat with his hand. He swallowed hard, twice. There was no trace of pain. Perhaps this was only a lull in the infection. Perhaps he was too numb to feel it. But it somehow seemed instead that the sickness had vanished altogether. If so, how? He could remember almost nothing from the delirium of the night before, but he seemed to recall the arrival of two men. Had they been doctors or healers? Even if they had, was Mirrorvaxan medical technology advanced enough to cure him?

The obvious answer was yes. Whether by drug or treatment, Michael was no longer ill. He was no longer in any pain. Yet the notion that they had saved him chilled him as well as comforted him. Either they had stumbled onto a wonder drug or their society was more advanced than he had guessed. Perhaps this settlement was less representative of Mirrorvax than he had supposed. Maybe there were great cities and centers of learning, industrial areas packed with technology, all of which might defy Transvax conquest. Two races, even, might exist on the planet, one ignorant and servile and the other advanced and dominant. A second highly developed race would explain how he had been cured and also how some of the natives had known to reach the AOT shortly after it landed. His heart began to pump faster. If the more advanced race had cured him, it might soon claim him, too.

Propping himself up, he tried to question Anamandra on the subject when she returned with a tray from the kitchen. His broken Mirrorvaxan bolstered by carefully articulated Vaxan terms meant nothing to her, however; she laughed as if he were trying to entertain her with nonsense. He must master the language enough to ask her about his cure, he decided. It was important to have accurate information about Mirrorvaxan technology when he returned to the ship. Turning to the food, he ate what Anamandra brought him with some difficulty. Non-synthetic eggs and a pale, hashed vegetable had too intense a taste for his liking. The frothy white liquid in a mug he was sure came from the cows. He found a warm, pasty substance in a bowl more to his liking, and he began to eat it while Anamandra went into the kitchen to take the baby from her mother.

When she returned, the overbundled small child in her arms, she laughed. "Maicyl," she said, "don't you want milk and honey with your porridge?" He swallowed, not exactly sure what she meant. The baby peered at him over the rim of the blanket. It blinked whenever he glared at it.

All along, Michael felt, he had been doing his best to understand Mirrorvaxan society, primitive though it was. After all, the Director had given clear instructions: he was to note every fact that might be important to the success of the mission. And since he had no voice-tape or notation pad, he had to do as best he could without them. But the natives, the more he knew about them, made increasingly less sense. He was even puzzled about his own mixed re-actions to them. And after breakfast, things grew more confused. The baby began to howl, so Anamandra took it upstairs, where it continued to cry for some time. Katandra Amudsar drifted in, felt his forehead, and asked him if he wanted her to contact his parents. No sooner had she gone, to "see to the garden," then Elissa arrived, stared at him, giggled, then went outside, where he saw her frolicking with the smelly animals someone had called dogs.

Aric and Corbi came in, red-cheeked, with buckets of the white liquid, which they took into the kitchen. One of them brought in a red-skinned fruit, which he rubbed against the sleeve of his shirt before handing it to Michael. They seemed to know his name and seemed interested in the fact that he was foreign. After they asked how he felt, Aric wanted to know what kind of clothes Michael had on. His reply was awkward. He was not sure it made sense, but it seemed to satisfy them. Corbi asked him to say something in his own language, and when he did, both of the boys laughed. Dis-covering he was laughing with them, Michael put his fingers on his lips. Corbi began to tell him about cows, and Aric went outside, then returned with a tree branch, which he broke and carved with a small-bladed knife, all the while telling Michael that this was the way to make a boat that would beat every other if you raced it in the canal. Before Aric had finished whittling the stick, however, his mother returned and scolded him for getting shavings on the carpet. When the two of them were gone, Michael picked up a cutting they had missed and held it in the light. One of the ship-board computers would be able to analyze the fineness of the cut and tell what kind of technology had produced the knife blade. Michael tucked it away in a leg pocket of his spacesuit.

At midday Michael ate a meal in the kitchen with the others, all gathered around a crudely crafted table. The food, he saw, was cooked on a primitive iron stove in matching soot-black kettles. The food—a variation of broth with vegetable bits in it—was more palatable than breakfast had been. Or it might have been, if Anamandra and Elissa, who had fought to win seats beside him, had not constantly peered at him over their spoons.

During the meal, Anamandra's mother asked Michael if he would care to change into cooler clothing. The spacesuit had indeed been hot and cumbersome, but Michael would not have parted with his last connection to the *AOT* even if shedding his suit had not been against regulations. He refused the offer with a shake of his head.

"He isn't terribly polite, is he?" Elissa whispered loudly to Corbi.

"He doesn't understand very much of what we say," Anamandra's mother said. "And he speaks our language even less well. Elissa, remember; he is foreign—"

"I *know*," Elissa said. "I keep hearing that. But what I wonder is how he got as far as our canal without being able to understand our language."

"El is right," Corbi said. "I've wondered the same thing. There are only a few foreigners, even in Snowhold, and Snowhold is too far away for him to have just wandered here."

"He didn't have to come from Snowhold," Anamandra

suggested. "Rush Valley may be far from anywhere else, but it isn't that far."

"But why would he come here?" Elissa asked.

Anamandra shrugged. She looked at her bowl. "He might be looking for work."

"Work," Michael said in hope of fortifying what looked like a feasible ruse. He cleared his throat. "I have come for work."

"See?" Anamandra said. She smiled at him. "Maicyl is looking for work."

"He can do *my* work for me," Aric said under his breath.

"Don't look at me as if you expect me to hire him, Ana," Katandra Amudsar said. "It's true your father has been looking for hired help since Imrand Wolscot began farming with his family. But that is your father's business, not mine. If Maicyl is still here when your father returns from Snowhold, and if Maicyl himself wants to work for us, that will be something between the two of them. Understand, Anamandra?"

She nodded, averting her eyes. But when she saw Michael's smile, she grinned. He, however, smiled not at the possibility of the proposition but at the absurdity of it. This family, apparently, was talking about buying him, as a Conglomerate would on Vax. At least that was what he presumed they meant by "hire." But they might find his price too high for them: Transvax had bought him for two thousand chronas, more than thirty work-lives. They would have to far surpass that to shake his loyalty to the Director's Space Operations Corporation, which, even beyond chronas, had invested lives and trust in him. Looking around the table, he laughed under his breath: he would soon escape—it would be simple to do so with these natives as his guards. And when he returned to this place, it would be to guide Space Corporation colonists.

That afternoon Anamandra took him into the yard, where she began the naming game they had played the day before.

But this time the words were names of animals, birds, buildings, trees, and mountains. A few of them seemed to be proper names. Rush Valley, for example, was the name Anamandra gave the basin between the hills. Michael found himself now able to form at least simple sentences. He wished the Director could have seen his striking progress, for although the language was relatively simple, remembering its vocabulary was not easy. And constant distractions—the buzzing translator, the smell and noise of the animals—made it difficult for him to concentrate. Anamandra, in addition, was not as patient a teacher as she perhaps thought. She often lapsed into long, rushed sentences that even the translating device had trouble following. At such times Anamandra's language was like music; with such a pleasant voice, in the new Mirrorvax, she might become a telescreen operator, if she could master Vaxan.

When they had finished touring the second barn, they stood near the gate to the yard and looked off across the valley. The sun was setting over the mountains where the AOT had landed. "We have beautiful sunsets in Rush Valley," Anamandra said. "You will grow to love them, if you stay here." Her eyes mirrored the painted clouds as she smiled at him. "The sky looks as if it is on fire, doesn't it, all flaming with red. The mountains turn the color of ashes, and then, as if the fire had burned them all up, the sunset goes cool and purplish, just as a fire does. Then there are only coals left in the sky, some of them glowing just faintly, so you can barely glimpse them. Those are the stars."

Stars, Michael wanted to tell her, were flaming balls of gas like the sun, massive galactic furnaces, hardly coals. Anamandra would learn that some day, one way or another. But in the meantime, he thought suddenly, her notion might not hurt. It was not a sensible observation, but the more he looked at the sky, the more he saw how she had made it. The sun flickered in the clouds, glittering like a ball of flame as it set. And when the first few stars pricked out, they were faint and reddish. He had never looked at them quite that way before.

"Look," Anamandra said, pointing, "a falling star!" A thread of light ran down the sky. It was nearly gone by the time he spotted it.

"A meteorite," Michael corrected in his own language.

"The Revelator says a falling star is a promise," Anamandra said. "He says that at the beginning of the world, stars fell, and that if the world must end, stars will fall again. But more often a falling star is a sign that He is giving someone a gift. I wonder who that someone might be."

At the evening meal Katandra Amudsar announced that she had heard from Anamandra's father and that Michael was welcome to stay at least until he returned from Snowhold. Michael wanted to ask her how she had heard, but he did not have the vocabulary. He had seen no messenger come during the day, and his examination of the farmyard had told him that the planet's technology was far too primitive for any kind of electronic communication. But perhaps he had been mistaken. Perhaps the natives had advanced communication. He resolved to stay with the family long enough to analyze the absolute level of Mirrorvaxan advancement. He must be accurate in his report to Transvax.

Logically, his first goal was to learn the language. At least to a degree that would let him ask Anamandra (whom he was now sure suspected nothing of his intentions) important questions. The possibility of a second race and advanced communication nagged at him the next few days, as Anamandra worked to teach him her language. They soon ran out of objects to name, so they began talking about more abstract things. Michael often had difficulty understanding what Anamandra said, even once it had been translated. The main difference between her culture and his, he determined, had to do with views on life, indeed on the universe. Anamandra's attitudes toward her home, her family, and her world were far more puzzling than her language. He did not pretend to understand them or even bother to. And he returned very few of his own perceptions, mostly because he constantly struggled for vocabulary. He came to the conclusion that Anamandra's complex misconceptions arose not from lack of intelligence, but from growing up in her primitive, family-structured society. How could she be logical when no one around her was? Indeed, even as they talked, sitting under the trees or on stumps by the barn, Anamandra's brothers would throw dirt clods at each other or entangle themselves in the branches of the trees, singing while hanging upside down. Elissa found every opportunity to pass by them, simpering, giggling, or raising her eyebrows at Anamandra. Michael soon thought that Anamandra had done well to become as rational as she was. She would make a respectable Vaxan, with proper training.

He had never before preferred one person over another. At least he had never admitted doing so. But he began to prefer Anamandra, at least over her younger siblings.

He also, strangely enough, began to prefer certain kinds of Mirrorvaxan food. He did not like the liquid that came from the cows. But he took a fancy to the round, greenish seeds he and Anamandra gathered from the garden one afternoon. Perhaps it was because Vaxan cleanliness had at least played part in their preparation. On the fourth day, he found himself requesting them for breakfast. This made Anamandra laugh for most of the morning. Laughing meant nothing, of course, but he began to care that Anamandra laugh when he did and not when he didn't.

In spite of the time he was committing to learning the language, he kept his mind open to other kinds of observations. And when Anamandra's mother called her in to take care of the baby or prepare a meal, he wandered around the yard taking samples of anything he thought might prove useful in analysis. He filled the pouches of his spacesuit with stones, seeds, shavings, twigs, bits of wire, dog hair, shreds of cloth, and leaves. He even took an egg from the shelter for the birds, whose name he could not remember. He regretted the act when his knee pocket soon became unusable. He also took samples of the green seeds but ate them raw a few hours later. He shuddered to imagine what the Director would say about eating samples, and he resolved that he would very soon go back to the ship. Jeremy by this time undoubtedly thought he was dead or captured. But Jeremy would understand the delay when Michael returned with a wealth of information about Mirrorvax. What better way was there to learn about the natives than to live with them for a time? Michael was sure the Director would approve of what he was doing and would be pleased when Michael reported all he had found to the Space Operations Corporation.

It had been chilling, at first, to wake at night on the couch, to see the odd shapes of things in the darkness, and to realize he was on a strange planet, in the custody of aliens. But somehow by the end of the fourth day, he no longer thought of any of them as aliens, particularly Anamandra. Anamandra, in fact, did not even seem to be a Mirrorvaxan. "If you were auctioned and I was a Conglomerate computer," he told her once, in his own language, "I would buy you. You would be a profitable asset." She would never have understood such a statement even in her own language, of course, much less in his, even though she had learned a few words of it. She only cocked her head to one side, spilling her wheat-colored hair, and smiled at him.

On the sixth day, Anamandra put food in a basket, and she and Michael went to the far end of the farm, to a grassy place beneath trees that overgrew the canal, to eat. The brush-covered hills rose at their backs, and seeing this was a perfect opportunity to escape, Michael tensed. He glanced back at the mountains so often that Anamandra asked him if anything was wrong. At last he decided he still did not have enough information to go back, so he settled comfortably in the shade and began to eat. Watching the sun glitter on the canal, he at last managed to ask Anamandra, in halting terms, how he had been cured of his illness.

"Brother Wolscot and Imrand did it," she said, as if

137

surprised by his question.

"But how?" Michael asked. "How?"

"With the Authority," she said. He presumed she meant authorization to use some kind of drug or technique. Perhaps from the more advanced race. He asked her from whom this Authority came. She told him to stop teasing her, he must know. He said he did not and asked again.

"From Him, of course," she said.

"From whom?"

"From Him," she repeated.

Michael sighed. "Who is he? What is his name?"

"He is Himself. He is He-Whose-Name-Is-Too-Sacred-to-Speak."

This statement meant even less than her previous ones had, and Michael wondered if his translator was operating correctly. Surely this was some kind of superstitious nonsense the more advanced race had handed down to Anamandra's. It seemed clear, however, that they gave permission to use their technology only to certain members of the lower race—that was what Anamandra meant by the Authority. Or so he presumed. Changing his line of questioning, he asked her who was given the Authority.

"Many people," she said. "My father has it, and my mother has a form of it."

"Are there people who bring things to one who has the Authority?"

Anamandra seemed puzzled, but finally her eyes lit up and she said, "Oh, yes. But they don't come to us very often. They come to the Revelator."

"Who is the Revelator?" Michael asked, supposing the position to be an intermediate between the two races.

"Siwarth Cincura," she replied. "He is Ecclesiarch and Revelator."

"Where does Siwarth Cincura live?" he said.

"In Snowhold," she answered. "I thought you knew that."

Anamandra looked so puzzled, he decided to stop asking questions for the time being. He began eating a hard, red fruit and gazed over the fields toward the house and the barns, which were just visible on the horizon. A slight wind rippled the fresh grass, drawing sunny patterns on the field. Anamandra inched to the canal and dipped her finger in it.

"Don't drink that," Michael said. "The cows have been in it."

She looked at him and laughed. He laughed, too, though he didn't know why. He laughed more than he had ever done before, mostly because Anamandra began laughing so hard tears came down her face. "That's the first funny thing you've said on purpose," she told him. "And Corbi thought you were a dead-pan." Still chuckling, she moved to him, put a hand on his shoulder, and kissed his cheek. When she drew away, she was smiling. Michael reddened. He presumed this guesture was given to anyone who said something amusing, but there was something undignified about it, something that made blood rush to his cheeks, and something that kept him from looking at Anamandra straight on.

Seeing his reaction, she looked at her hands. She seemed suddenly unhappy. "The cows have been in it," he said again, tentatively.

"Speaking of the cows," Anamandra said, looking up at him, "I was supposed to take them to the south pasture. I . . . forgot to. Wait here, Maicyl, and I will be back." She stood up, glanced back at him, and hurried away. He sank his teeth into the fruit and watched her grow smaller on the road to the house, until she nearly disappeared. The odd behavior of the natives might always be beyond him, he thought as he gathered remnants of food and replaced them in the basket. Perhaps Anamandra was not as logically-motivated as he had thought. That she had left so suddenly gave him an odd sensation in his stomach. A very odd, inexplicable sensation. At any rate, there seemed no point in sitting beside the canal if she was not there to question. He ought to go back to the farm and collect more samples.

Taking the basket in his arm, he started back. He followed ruts beside a fence that Anamandra had said marked the boundary between her family's land and that of the Wolscots, their neighbors. The ruts seemed to have been made by some kind of wheeled vehicle, probably very primitive, and Michael was so busy trying to determine what kind of device might be responsible that he did not notice the man until a shadow fell across the rut.

The man, dressed as Anamandra's brothers had been, sat on top of a fencepost, legs balanced on the wires of the fence, arms folded. He glared at Michael with charcoal-colored eyes, which under a shaggy mane of light brown hair, made him look like a statue of a lion Michael had once seen in the ruins of a Vaxan imperial palace. He had a very straight, sharp nose and tight lips. He seemed young but fierce, and his shoulders, work-hardened, were knotted and grooved. He stepped down from the fence when Michael reached him. "Hello," he said. He glanced at the basket. "Been picnicking?"

That was the term Anamandra had used. "Yes," he said.

"With Anamandra, I saw," he said.

"Yes," Michael said.

"Who are you, anyway? Where do you come from?"

Michael was not sure how to answer these questions convincingly; the family had simply accepted him as a foreigner, so he had never really had to explain himself. He was not sure he could now, not in the Mirrorvaxan language, so he resorted to an expression he had often heard Anamandra use with Elissa. "It isn't any of your business."

The young man's scowl only deepened. "I'll tell you who I am, foreigner. I am Imrand Wolscot. I have lived in this valley longer than you have, and I even worked at the Amudsars' for two years. And one thing you ought to know before you go on any more picnics with Anamandra is that she is spoken for!"

Michael wanted to ask who had spoken for her. But though what Imrand Wolscot said made little sense to him, he could see that the man was becoming more belligerent. Michael surely could not tolerate such blunt insubordination from a creature who was so obviously his inferior. The only sensible thing to do was walk away. He started to, but as he moved past Imrand Wolscot, the basket banged against the man's flank. The next thing Michael knew, a full fist landed in his stomach. The spacesuit absorbed most of the blow, but it took his breath just the same. Dropping the basket, he doubled forward. In a sudden burst of rage, he tackled Imrand's leg and toppled him to the ground. Imrand punched at him again, then he struggled to his haunches, leaped aside, then pushed Michael to the ground, where he pinned him down at his shoulders and sat on his chest. He jabbed his fist beneath Michael's chin and said through set teeth, "Take it easy."

Michael seemed to have no choice. This brawny native was far stronger than he was. "You're a nice example of a savage society," Michael growled, in his own language. "We'll file unruly native reports on people like you! We could vaporize you at a moment's notice, and level your whole filthy planet in a day! Perhaps we shall. Perhaps I'll suggest it when I go back to Vax! Get off me, dog!"

"Jeer at me in your barbarian language, will you?" Imrand said. He stood up, kicked at Michael, then vaulted the fence. From the other side he sneered back, "You're not even worth roughing up. But remember what I said. Anamandra has been spoken for. Keep that in your head." Then he vanished into the bushes on the far side of the fence.

Michael stood up, brushed himself off, and gathered up what had spilled from the basket. "Filthy alien," he muttered to himself as he started down the road. His cheeks felt as hot as they had the day Judy had first called him recyclage. To have his dignity bruised by one who was his equal had been bad enough, but to be insulted and humiliated by a half-naked, unwashed native, without any provocation, infuriated him. Perhaps he *would* file an unruly native report. It would be good to see these grubby natives and their paltry society go up in artillery smoke. Perhaps he would personally take revenge on Imrand Wolscot. And perhaps he would return to the ship that very day. He stifled an urge to start back to the ship that very moment; he must at least ask Anamandra a question or two before he left.

Yet his wounded pride made him taciturn for the rest of the day. He did not see Anamandra most of the afternoon and instead spent his time gathering samples and nursing his rage. He phrased half his report to the Secretariat while picking his way through the vegetable garden, collecting seeds and leaves. He would not suggest total destruction of the society, he decided, but he would support use of artillery and death-cords to eliminate ugly buildings and unruly natives.

Anamandra sat next to him at dinner, but she hardly looked at him, and spoke to him only when one of the others did. To occupy herself, she took the baby from her mother and balanced it on her lap, looping an arm around its waist to keep it from tipping over. The baby, however, watched Michael's every movement with a wide-open mouth. Its expression was so silly and the movement of its head so jerky that Michael found himself smiling. The baby, unexpectedly, smiled back; a wide, toothless, open-mouthed smile that instantly disarmed him. He prodded its stomach, as he had seen Elissa do. It gooed and smiled again. Anamandra looked at him just when he had made a face to amuse the baby. She laughed. "I think Diafana likes you," she said. "Would you like to hold her?"

Before he could answer, he found Diafana dumped in his lap. Anamandra helped him hook an arm around her. The baby laid its head back against his chest and peered up at him. All he could think of to do was to hold it stiffly and say hello to it. "Diafana won't break," Anamandra told him. The baby gooed again.

Even when he had returned the baby to Anamandra, a warm, sticky kind of feeling remained in his stomach, and his eyes burned as if he had gotten dust in them until he went to bed on the couch. All he could think of, as he stared into the darkness and listened to the creak of the house in the wind, was the baby's laughter and Anamandra's smile. He found both of them unsettling because of the odd notions of warmth they gave him. He knew he must push them from his mind, they were obviously primitive sensations; but he could not manage to do so until he had decided that he would not start back to the ship right away, after all. And the colonists would certainly have to do without artillery when they came.

With such thoughts he grew drowsy. The voices of Anamandra and her family threaded through his mind, growing fainter as he lapsed toward sleep. But then a voice, cold and hard like steel, buzzed in the microphone of his translator and made him sit bolt upright. "Michael? Michael? Can you hear me? I know you aren't expecting this. This is *The Arm of Transvax*. This is Judy."

VOICES
FROM DARKNESS

THE DARKNESS of the room seemed to spin as Michael stood up. "Judy!" he cried out, his voice hoarse, his eyes combing the darkness for some sign of her. But her voice spoke in the hollow of his ear, not from the room. It continued, uninterrupted by his outburst. "We understand that you cannot reply. There is no way we can hear you. But we hope that, wherever you are, you can hear us. Jeremy has been working for days to set up a transmitter that will broadcast to your translator, and we have taken the risk that one of the natives may have captured your translating device and may be listening. Our surveys indicate native technology will not let them locate us by our transmission, and we know that none of them speak our language. Michael, listen. We hope you can listen. We are taking the chance that you can, even though Jeremy's sensor-scope picked up an explosion a number of days ago that might have been your short-barrel."

"Judy," Michael muttered, sinking to a seat on the sofa. He tucked the audiophone deeper in his ear, afraid he might miss something she said. He wanted to answer her, to tell her where he was and what he was doing, to ask her how she had returned to the ship. Feeling muzzled, he listened hungrily.

"If you can hear me, your most urgent problem may be Mirrorvaxan bacteria. Whatever you do, do not take off your filter, and do not drink Mirrorvaxan water without first sterilizing it with the Medron purifiers in your survival kit." Michael patted his breast pocket; he had never even opened the kit. Indeed, he had forgotten about it for the first day and a half of his stay. "We hope you have taken all the proper precautions, because if you have not, I am speaking to darkness; Mirrorvaxan microbes are lethal to us because our bodies have built up no defenses against them. I lost my mask when I was first captured by the natives, and if I had not escaped and returned to the ship by nightfall, Jeremy would not have been able to save me. Even our most advanced antibiotics helped only a little, and to develop a vaccine serum takes hours, if not days. Both Jeremy and I are fully immune to what bacteria we have been able to isolate. But Michael, if you can hear me, it is absolutely imperative that you return to the ship to receive vaccination. We fear the worst, because the bacteria kills in an estimated thirty hours. We would have warned you sooner, but we were busying saving our own lives and building this transmitter."

Bacteria, Michael thought, swallowing. He had been seriously infected when Anamandra had first found him; and from what Judy had said, he should have been dead that first evening. He had taken off his filter and drunk Mirrorvaxan water. He had even eaten Mirrorvaxan food. And except for an odd knot in his stomach, he felt perfectly healthy now. The Mirrorvaxans had somehow outdone Vaxan medicine and saved him. But how? That was something he would have to discover.

"Jeremy and I have determined that you went after me when I got lost," Judy went on. "Again, we suspect the worst, because each of us has searched the landing area with no sign of you. If you have been captured, and if your captors took off your filter, as mine did, you are lost to us. I nearly was, as I have said. The natives, a group of half a dozen of them, surprised me. They seemed to have been waiting for me for a long time, because they were well-stationed for an ambush. I killed one of their number with a death-coil, but the rest of them disarmed me of my cords and marched me away. I couldn't understand their language, but they seemed primitive and hostile. I believe they planned to kill me eventually. But though they took death-cords from me, they did not take the venom-eggs. So before we had gone far, I slipped a few out and escaped in the confusion caused by killing at least one more of them."

Michael swallowed and touched his finger to his ear. He should have known Judy would be able to take care of herself. He should have gone back to the ship.

A click followed; Michael feared the transmission had ended. But Jeremy's voice sounded in his ear, as thick and hoarse as Michael remembered it. "Michael, we know that you made a mistake in trying to follow Judy. But that no longer matters. What matters is that, if you are able, you return to the ship as soon as possible. We have fended off two native attack groups with artillery. None of them seemed armed, and none of them were large, but we expect a bigger attack soon. If we become surrounded, we may have no choice but to launch; this mission was designed to be scientific, not military, and though a single Vaxan guard unit with short-barrels could probably level this planet's civilization, there are only two of us here. We have gathered vegetation and animal samples, taken photographs and sensor surveys; and we have samples of Mirrorvaxan technology from natives that our artillery have killed. We have nearly enough information, we think, to enable the Space Operations Corporation to plan a colonizing mission. Or we will have in a few days. If we are under attack at that time, we will lift off. I repeat: return as soon as possible. If you do not, or if we do not receive some sign that you are alive, we cannot wait for you. That is all for now."

The translator then fell silent, except for its customary low-pitched buzz. But the two voices echoed in Michael's mind; he had to go back. Pictures of Judy and Jeremy and the Director raced through his mind as he stood up. He glanced at the door, then through the window at the darkness beyond. He fastened the throat of his suit, then crept toward the door. But even when his fingers found the latch, he didn't open it. He hesitated, listening to the rhythmic squeak of floorboards. He heard the Mirrorvaxan wind humming in the trees beyond the porch. He smelled bread in the darkness; Anamandra had shown him how she made it before he had gone to bed.

A sudden pang, a kind of stiffness in his stomach that he had never felt before, gripped him. He tried to open the door, but he could not bring himself to. His eyes felt inexplicably hot. "Anamandra," he whispered, flattening a hand against the stomach of his suit. "Anamandra."

"I'm here," a voice whispered back. A shape emerged from the shadows of the kitchen. When the pale light from the window struck her robe and nightgown, Anamandra reached toward him. He backed against the door. "I'm sorry to startle you," she murmured. "I thought you knew I was here. I came down when I heard you shout. I thought you might be having a nightmare. I thought you might be sick again."

"Not sick," he said, trying to master unaccountable fear. "Nightmare."

"Anything it would help to tell me?" she said.

"No," he said. "No."

She moved toward him, but she held herself back when she glimpsed his hand on the doorknob. "Are you going somewhere?" she asked.

"Air," he said. "I need air."

"I'll come out with you, then," she said. "I could use some fresh air, too."

When both of them stood on the porch, light from the

craggy Mirrorvaxan moon let Michael see Anamandra's face. It was taut, perhaps because of the wind that trailed her hair away and made the hem of her robe beat against one of the doorposts. But her eyes seemed to glow faintly as she looked at him. Her frown deepened as she stepped off the porch.

He forced himself to turn around and look at her. "Anamandra," he said. He fought for breath in the face of the wind. "Anamandra, I—" She curled her arm around a post, and part of the glitter that had been in her eyes began to edge down her cheek. "Anamandra," he said for a third time, wrenched by something he did not understand and could never hope to, something that made him feel empty and stung and warm and confused all at the same time. But then he took something from his pocket, and keeping his eyes on her, he backed away into the yard. The wind knocked against him, and the tossing of the dark branches hid Anamandra by the time he reached open ground.

He knelt and anchored the thing in the dust, fished in his pocket for a palm-sized metal object, which he brought to a cord attached to the top of the object he had put in the dust. A flame sprang from the metal box and burned down the cord, in spite of the wind. Michael sprang back. He reached cover of the trees by the time the flare shot up a plume of blue fire. Sparks lit the house and the barn. They climbed skyward in a glittering spiral; the wind smudged them into a trail of fire that descended slowly over the neighboring fields like a falling star. When the last blue shards of fire roosted in the trees beyond the pasture and went dark, Michael returned to the porch.

Anamandra's eyes were wide. "I . . . I don't understand," she said.

"A flare," he said in his own language. "A flare to tell Jeremy and Judy I am still alive." He looked at her. "A flare to tell them I won't be going back to the ship immediately." As the flare had done, the fire inside him began to die as he took Anamandra inside. But a stab of guilt, followed by flashes of the Director's face, made him promise himself he would return to *The Arm of Transvax* very soon. But for some reason, Anamandra's puzzled look justified his delay. Not knowing why he did so, he took her hand, cold from the wind, and pressed it between his palms. He bowed his head toward hers, to fathom the sparkle of refracted moonlight on her eyes.

But sounds of footsteps from the kitchen made him pull away. Katandra Amudsar, surrounded by wide-eyed children, appeared in the doorway. There was a giggle, probably from Elissa. "Hm," Corbi's voice said. "I think we know why all of us saw fireworks."

Anamandra's hand wriggled from Michael's grasp. "I just came down to make sure Maicyl was all right. He seemed to be having a nightmare."

"Fortunately for all of us, Anamandra," her mother said, "your father will be home tomorrow."

Toward morning, Michael's dreams of canals and trees were shattered by Judy's voice in his translator. She said they had spotted a disturbance on their thermoscope record that seemed to have come moments after their broadcast; because the heat disturbance appeared to have the dimensions of a Vaxan flare, they considered it a signal that Michael was still alive. But the suits were outfitted with two flares; Judy said that if Michael was indeed all right and able to do so, he should send his second flare. Wild with relief, Michael left the house. Faint hints of dawn brushed up in the sky beyond the mountains, and the wind had died down. He went farther from the house this time, nearly to the canal, before he knelt and stationed the flare on the ground. But as he took his ignitor from his pocket, he hesitated. He thought of Anamandra and suddenly wished, though he could not explain why, that Judy and Jeremy would think he was dead. He somehow wanted them to return to Vax without him.

He thought this only because he was still half asleep, he

149

soon reasoned. Why would he want to stay on this primitive planet, with ignorant natives? Why did something make him want to be with Anamandra? She was simply another native. He lit the flare and moved away. But he bit his lip when flame shot up, paling the last few stars into obscurity. And he was almost sorry to hear Judy's acknowledgement of his signal as he walked back to the house.

"We are now assuming you to be alive," she said. It might be a trick of static, but she sounded almost excited. "Please return as soon as possible. Repeat: as soon as possible." Michael knew the order came from Jeremy. And he knew that the Director had said he must obey Jeremy. He lingered at the barn, glancing at the mountains where the AOT lay. But he must wait here a little longer, he told himself. He must ask Anamandra how her people had kept him from death.

Yet when the house awoke and Anamandra came down to prepare breakfast, he almost forgot about asking her. After all, she had not seemed to know much about the subject before. The only person who seemed to know more than Anamandra was her mother, but because of the looks she gave them that morning, Michael dared not ask her anything.

"Father will be back today—soon," Anamandra told him as she placed utensils on the table. "You will like my father very much, I think. And I'm sure he will like you just as much."

Michael himself could see no reason why he should like Anamandra's father, or he him. But he suspected her father would have more answers to his questions than Anamandra did.

After breakfast Anamandra suggested that they go on a walk. Anamandra's mother instructed Aric to go along with them. Michael could see no purpose in this, and he was somehow irked by Aric's presence. They walked along the canals without saying very much until Anamandra said they ought to visit the Wolscots, whose farm they had come near. Remembering his scuffle with Imrand, Michael was not in favor of visiting at all; but when he remembered that the older Wolscot man had the Authority, he decided the other farm might be worth investigating.

Thiand Wolscot, the father, however, was not home. Neither was Imrand; the woman said both of them had gone to the far end of the valley, where Mandon Pedinsar, a representative of the Revelator, was organizing some kind of search operation. But they sat down in a living room very different from the Amudsars', and Michael met Conat, Imrand's younger brother but almost his twin, and Azura, a slender girl with a scar on her cheek, who served him sweet, crunchy things from a plate. Even with the translator and his increased knowledge of Mirrorvaxan, he could hardly follow Anamandra and Cindra Wolscot's conversation about alien and unfamiliar things. But his visit to the second farm convinced him that the planet's technology was even more backward than he had thought. The Wolscot's house seemed both smaller and older than the Amudsars', and they kept far fewer animals.

When they had come scarcely halfway back from the Wolscot farm, Anamandra said she saw dust on the Snowhold road. She pointed into the distance, but Michael saw nothing. By the time they crossed the canals and started across the pasture, though, Anamandra said the dust was gone. She had imagined it, she said, or else her father had come home. "I see the wagon," Aric said when they had come halfway across the pastures. "And there are people standing in the yard, under the trees."

The wagon, Michael saw as they approached, was as primitive a means of transportation as he had expected. No more than a crudely made wooden box fitted with four wooden-spoke wheels, it was drawn by two of the creatures Anamandra had called horses. The two beasts, both dirty white, jostled and shook their heads; their strappings were tied to a tree. The wagon itself, including a bench at its front probably meant to be a seat, was empty. But near the porch Anamandra's mother and her siblings gathered around a tall man who faced away from Michael. A second man, apparently older than the first, stood a little to the side, smiling absently. After they passed the first barn, both Anamandra and Aric broke into a run. Michael saw them each embrace the tall man and took up a position at the edge of the trees. Somehow he felt threatened, though logic told him he had nothing to fear from either of the men.

"This is my youngest son, Aric," the tall man shouted to the other, taking one of his children under each arm. "And this is Anamandra, my oldest daughter. This, both of you, is Elder Talis Ratham, from the Ecclesiat."

The second man beamed at them, round-faced. "I've never met anyone from the Ecclesiat," Corbi muttered to his father. "Why has he come here?"

Anamandra's father said something Michael could not hear. Anamandra, meanwhile, broke away from her family and moved to Michael. She took him by the sleeve and drew him toward her father. "I have someone you should meet, Father," she said. "This is Maicyl Tuwin, the man Mother has told you about. Maicyl, this is my father, Lorloric Amudsar. And this is Elder Ratham."

Michael dropped his head at them, as he had when Anamandra had introduced him to the Wolscots. But he saw that after each had glanced at him, they looked at one another, and Ratham nodded slightly. When Lorloric Amudsar looked back at him, Michael noticed how very much like Anamandra's his eyes were, mirror-black and fathomless. But he read something more in Lorloric Amudsar's eyes than he had in Anamandra's, something that made him feel suddenly cold. It was as if the big-framed man, dressed in a uniform of dark cloth, hair cloud-gray and thick, face weather-lined and sunburned, was not a human at all, but the representative of some star-old and wise people, some stern and powerful race that had mastered the universe. The other man had the same look, but it did not bother Michael as much; the eerie thing was that Amudsar, for all his majesty, still looked like Anamandra's father.

"Sister Amudsar," Ratham said to Anamandra, "we really don't need to be introduced to your friend."

"Michael is the reason Elder Ratham has come," Anamandra's father said.

"Why has he come for me?" Michael said, gripping Anamandra's arm. "Why?" His spine prickled. He could look neither of the men in the eye.

"We would like you to travel to Snowhold with us, if you will please consider it," Ratham said. "We would like you to meet the Revelator."

The fact that the Revelator might be able to give him information no longer seemed important; Michael felt dread overwhelm him. "Why?" he almost shouted. "Why?"

"Because the Revelator wants to speak with you, Michael," Anamandra's father said. "Because, Michael of Counter-earth, we know who you are, where you came from, and why you have come to Mirrorvax."

SNOWHOLD

BEFORE NOON, Rush Valley disappeared as the walls of the canyon closed in. Michael watched the range of mountains where the *AOT* had landed fade behind a wall of cloud. He watched the house and the two barns sink into the horizon. Then, as he road wound into the hills, walls of pale rock cropped up to hide the valley from him completely. Snowhold was not far, Anamandra's father had said. They would arrive there by early afternoon, in spite of the slow pace of the wagon. Dread, however, the hollow burning Michael had had in his stomach ever since he had seen Anamandra's father, made the pace seem swifter. Bends in the double-rut road came swiftly, and rock faces flanked by the tall, feathery fern-trees seemed to flash by.

He did not know why he had agreed to go to Snowhold. In fact, he was not sure he had agreed. He had simply climbed onto the wagon seat between Talis Ratham and Lorloric Amudsar as soon as Anamandra's mother had put together food for their journey. It had occurred to him to run. Actually, he almost had when Anamandra's father had used the word *Mirrorvax*. He knew he could have escaped; he was, after all, faster than the older men and stronger than the boys. But something had made him stand his ground. The same something was taking him to Snowhold.

Now that his mind had begun to clear, he saw that he had at least two good reasons for letting the men take him, in spite of the obvious risks involved. To begin with, Anamandra seemed to think it was a good thing for him to do. She had been as shocked as he had by what her father had said, though she certainly understood less of its implications. But seeing his fear, she whispered to him that it would be all right, that neither her Father nor the Revelator meant him harm. Anamandra did not seem to understand as much as her father did, and her assumption seemed naive. If the men knew who he was and why he had come, they would not only want to harm him but probably to kill him. Still, Anamandra had clung to his arm while her parents made preparations for the trip; and when he had left, she had waved to him. The logic of this defied him; but somehow he found what she had done for him more comforting than any of his reasoning.

The only logical reason he had for cooperating made his skin crawl. The whole purpose of his mission here, as he had muttered to himself time and time again since the journey began, was to gather information. Information that would be useful to Transvax in planning conquest of this planet. That meant he must explore anything that might be a threat to that conquest. And the knowledge Anamandra's father and the other man seemed to have about him was the most dangerous thing he had faced yet. How did they know, for instance, that he had come from another world? What Michael had seen of their society seemed too primitive to undertake serious astronomy. And even educated people on Vax would never guess that a Mirrorvaxan, if he were placed in Helcar or Valacar, came from another world. More, how had they learned what his mission was? Or were they bluffing? If so, how did they know the name of their own planet in *his* language? He had never taught even Anamandra that.

His first notion was that they or their compatriots had

learned the word from Judy. But Judy had been away from the spaceship for only a day. And her contact with the natives had been without a translator. They could have been monitoring Judy's broadcasts, but he had yet to see any device more sophisticated than wheels or wire. It was possible, of course, that Snowhold was an industrial and technological center, a place where life-saving drugs and radio receivers were made. But somehow that seemed unlikely. Somehow neither of the men seemed as if they had ever been associated with machines at all.

He sat between them, unmoving, as they rode. Both smelled of sun-warm fabric and dust, and both sat forward on the wagon seat, as if they had ridden in such a vehicle often. Their expressions remained constantly unreadable; they wore quiet half-smiles that deepened only when they exchanged a few words, when one of them spotted an animal or an unusual rock formation. But for the most part, both of them were uncannily quiet.

He supposed he should prepare himself to meet technology and to find that the Revelator they had mentioned was the key to a machine-operating aristocracy. Perhaps the man was a member of a second race, as he had thought before. But in reality he expected something else, something that he had never dreamed existed before he met Anamandra. He expected to meet a power in Snowhold that had little to do with technology or industry or even logic. A kind of power that he was only slowly becoming sensitive to, the kind of force one felt on Vax only accidentally or perhaps in child-bearing suburbs. It was something with the power to change the temperament of what was inside, to make one feel afraid or happy or angry or loved. He knew the terminology well enough: it had been part of the vocabulary in advocate curriculum. But these feelings—all of them —were primitive, savage, and often unpleasant. Vax had eliminated the need for them by creating a world so ordered no one need ever fear or love or become angry. It was because Mirrorvax was not so advanced that its inhabitants still had feelings, and according to what Michael had been taught, such vestiges of a primitive past only got in the way.

He, himself, had begun to understand these feelings— objectively. He had never actually *felt* any of them, of course. He was too civilized for that. But he had come to understand how powerful they were, in a savage kind of way. And he had an inkling that these very feelings might be the most dangerous adversaries colonists from Vax would meet. Because the feelings, he was sure, had something to do with the Revelator and his organization, though his power probably came from logic or technology.

Jeremy had known something about feelings. Perhaps he had even experienced them. But Jeremy was beyond reach now; the brief status reports from him and Judy were little help, and less comfort. And when they urged him to return to the ship, he found himself wishing he had escaped the night before. Why hadn't he? Why had he been so short-sighted?

For some reason he began to think about Anamandra. He found he could picture her face clearly; he captured the exact color of her hair, the precise curve of her lips, the particular sound of her laugh. As the canyon yielded to a hilltop forest, he remembered how he and Anamandra had talked beneath the trees. As the wagon bumped down the bottom of a river gorge, he recalled the day they had spent beside the canal. When Amudsar halted to let the horses drink from the stream, Michael reflected on the smell of the bread Anamandra had baked. He heartily wished her father had let her come along with them. After all, he told himself, she was the native with whom he could communicate best.

He soon put Anamandra's memory aside, however; in a few hours they emerged from the gorge into a valley very similar to the one where the Amudsars had their farm. Pale green foothills swept down to a flat valley floor bounded by steep mountains in the distance. Faint blue lines and regular green-and-brown rectangles indicated agriculture, and lines of trees seemed to parallel canals. Clumps of trees also marked houses and barns scattered over the valley bottom. A larger group of trees and buildings Michael at first mistook to be only a larger version of the same. But when Ratham caught sight of it, he nudged Michael and pointed. "Snowhold," he said.

The mass of trees seemed a little larger when the wagon jolted its way to the valley level. But Michael estimated the town could not extend more than a mile in any direction. Girded by fields, barns, and a river, it still resembled a farm settlement. No smokestack or broadcasting tower thrust above the trees. No wires, except those in fences, linked it with the outside. Michael saw no signs of landing pads or machinery or even large structures that might indicate technological development. The only building of any size, in fact, seemed to be a squarish white structure with six blunt spires that just edged above the trees, somewhere near the center of the town. Michael asked Anamandra's father if this was really Snowhold. He replied that it was. Michael tried to ask him whether part of it lay elsewhere or underground, but neither of the men seemed to understand the question. When he managed to ask them about other cities, Ratham only said, "Snowhold is the main city for this part of the world. There are others, over the sea: White Bay, Silverwood, Sandgold, and many more. All are different from Snowhold. Some are vast cities, for those who have chosen to live so. But all are much the same. All have temples: but Snowhold has the Revelator."

"Temple," Michael said. He squinted at the towers rising out of the trees. As the translator put the word in his language, it meant the ancient stone shrines the emperors of Old Vax had raised, when they believed in magic and conjuring. But that had been thousands of years ago on Vax. The Mirrorvaxan culture must be that many years behind, if they were as superstitious. Still, the building Lorloric Amudsar said was the temple did not seem massive or savage or imposing. That it was different from the Imperial Vaxan versions was clear; yet that was only a manifestation of a different culture. Michael hoped somehow that they would pass by it.

As they came to smoother roads and passed the first ring of trees, he became more confident. It seemed Snowhold was anything but a technological center. A single Transvax guard unit, armed with hand artillery, would be able to level the town in less than a day. Michael even thought of the strategy they might use to do so as the wagon crept toward the center of the town. If strategy would be needed at all. The streets of the town, if they could be called such, were broad but unpaved. Dust rose from the packed earth as other wagons lumbered along, laden with baskets of fruit or heaps of dried grass. The people weaving in among the wagons and horses were little better dressed than Anamandra's family had been. The women wore long robes, as Anamandra had; the men's dress was more varied but often in poorer condition. Teenage boys throwing spheres at one another in a grassy place between the houses wore no shirts and heavily patched trousers. The streets were congested with wagons, but it was not really crowded. The town was composed mostly of brightly painted houses, in the style of Anamandra's and only a little larger. Each house was surrounded by old trees and lawns or gardens, and separated from the street by pickets, usually painted white, often with a dog or small child peering through the slats. At one point they passed a grassy area framed by wagons and filled with colorful stands brimming with produce. The place was obviously a market; seemingly it was the town's main commercial center. Michael laughed, for only a few people, women with their baskets, walked among the stands. This would hardly be formidable trade opposition for Transvax, especially if this was the population center for part or all of a continent. None of what had been built here would even be useful to Transvax; the town would simply be evacuated and destroyed from the air. Indeed, most of the area of the town would be needed for a simple air-shuttle station.

They crossed a tree-shaded river by a stone bridge, and Michael found himself in a more closely packed quarter of the town. The streets here had been paved in stone, but roughly; and although many of the buildings were brick or stone, too, most of them seemed as primitive as their neighbors across the river. The buildings, most of them double-storied, came to the edge of the street. Some of them had big doors to admit wagons. Some seemed to be working places for artisans; Michael glimpsed a metal shop and a stone-cutting shop, both of which seemed backward. A few of the buildings had broad windows with signs over them; pairs of men and women drifted out of them. But though Michael could read none of the signs (indeed, he was surprised to discover that the Mirrorvaxan language could be written), he knew what the buildings were. They were rudimentary trade establishments, pale shadows of the great Vaxan Conglomerate organizations. Though any comparison between these shops and Transvax or Syntac was obviously absurd.

Before long the street approached the building Ratham had called the temple. Like the houses on the outskirts of the town, it was surrounded by old trees and lawns. These were separated from the street by an iron-slat fence with stone pillars that matched the masonry of the building. From what he could see of it through the trees, it was bigger than he had before guessed, both heavier and taller. Thick buttresses supported the six white towers, three of them at each end of the structure; the tallest tower peaked in a triangle of gold that was blinding to look at. But although the building was the most striking example of Mirrorvaxan architecture Michael had seen, it seemed no more advanced than the stone houses, and he doubted if it housed a technological control center, as he had before suspected.

"What is this building for?" he asked Anamandra's father.

"It is a house," he replied, glancing at it. "His house."

"Whose house? The Revelator's?"

"No," he said. "The Revelator lives there." He pointed down the street toward a house built of the same stone as the temple and in somewhat the same style. "Siwarth Cincura, who has been the Revelator now for more years than my children can remember, lives there. He is often at the temple, but he will meet you in the upper room of his own home."

"What does the Revelator do?" Michael asked. Looking at the tree-obscured windows of the house, he swallowed hard. "Does he lead you?"

"He tells us what He would like us to do," Ratham replied.

The Revelator, then, was some kind of civic authority, Michael thought. Presumably he was the ruler of the area commercially controlled by Snowhold. That meant he corresponded to a member of the Transvax Secretariat or a judge on the Vaxan World Tribunal. But the comparison, of course, was hardly just. This man ruled a society so primitive that he was probably more like a savage chieftain than a Conglomerate executive. Michael laughed when he thought of the Secretariat complex at Helcar—a mass of some sixty skyscrapers, he had heard—then looked at the old stone house sleeping behind its garden.

Anamandra's father pulled the wagon to a stop in front of the gate. The horses stomped the pavement, and the one nearest the fence began nibbling at all stalks of grass that grew between the pickets. As Michael stepped down from the wagon, stiff-legged, he smelled newly cut grass and something sweet, like sun-warmed honey. The afternoon light striped across the garden, floodlighting flowerbeds and lawns and dropping thick shadows beneath the trees. A slight wind stirred the slender upper branches, making their reflections move back and forth across the big windows on the top floor. The place gave Michael a sensation of silence and age. He felt something else, too—something he could

161

almost hear—but he could not identify it.

"Come in with us," Ratham said. "The Revelator is waiting."

Only when they reached the porch did Michael begin to grow nervous again. He knew the men must want to harm him if they knew who he was, and their Revelator sounded more fierce every minute. Supposing he was more savage than his subjects? Or worse, supposing he was the key to the higher level of technology Michael still suspected might exist? He might kill Michael before Michael had a chance to gather information and escape. Yet since the only way to learn the final secrets of Mirrorvax seemed to be through meeting this man, Michael moved inside when Anamandra's father opened the door.

The inside of the house was dim, cool, and a little musty. Blue drapes masked the windows, and a blue and white carpet climbed a broad staircase. An old woman with thin, pale hair and a round, ruddy face met them. She seemed to know both men, for she acknowledged them with a nod and a smile before she turned to Michael. Her expression hardened, and her deep-set eyes kindled as she said, in almost a whisper, "Welcome to Snowhold, Michael of Counter-earth. We have been expecting you." She returned her glance momentarily to the other men. "Brother Ratham and Brother Amudsar, I hope you will make yourselves comfortable while I take him to see Ecclesiarch Cincura. It should not take too long."

To think why it might not made Michael more apprehensive than before. The two men took seats by the door, and the woman started up the stairs, picking up her skirts with a plump-knuckled hand. "If you will please follow me," she said. "The Revelator is waiting."

In spite of her apparent age, the woman climbed the steps with practiced agility, pausing on the landings only to check that Michael was following her. She said nothing to him, but her glances, cool and businesslike at first, grew sharper. She stole looks at him as if she were hungry for them—she seemed to notice his spacesuit, the color of his hair and eyes, the contours of his face, and the posture of his walk. But always she blinked, when he glared back, and looked away. A few times it seemed as if she wanted to ask him something, but she only pressed her lips and kept moving. When eight flights of stairs had passed, she paused at a dark wood door.

She knocked smartly; the sound boomed down the stairwell and seemed to echo beyond the door. Michael heard no response, but she opened the latch and motioned him in. When he had passed the threshold, she nodded at him and left the room, closing the door behind her.

Michael found himself in a U-shaped room, lit by windows at each of its extremities. Dark panels surrounded the semi-circular back of the room, broken by paintings of the town and the temple and the mountains. A wide desk, carpeted with papers and other oddments, took up most of the space of the room. And behind it, in a high-backed chair, was a man.

He was nothing like the man Michael had expected. He was not as imposing as Ratham or Anamandra's father, for he was hardly as big. Standing he would probably be little taller than the old woman, and he seemed near her age, if not older. He wore a suit something like Ratham's but plainer. He was almost bald, and what hair he had was so wispy and colorless that Michael could see age-speckled skin beneath it. His face seemed even rounder than the old woman's, mostly because of his bald pate. His face seemed redder and more lined, so much so that the man's features—a modest nose and pale lips—hardly stood out, and only his ears, conspicuous because of their size, and his eyes, conspicuous because of their color, stood out. The man seemed almost comic and hardly formidable as long as Michael avoided his eyes.

They were silver, as if they were plates of highly polished aluminum. All other eyes Michael had seen on Mirrorvax had been black and glossy; these seemed to have the same reflective qualities except that they were somehow deeper, as if they were mirrors turned partially inward. But more than that, they were windows, clear openings on a scene Michael could almost glimpse, a landscape of clouds and stars. When the man stood up, the light made them glitter. Michael felt pricked by each spark of light that shone from them.

"Michael," the man said. His voice was rough and deep, though not loud. "I am glad to see you here. I was almost afraid you would not come." In a horrifying rush, Michael realized that his translator had gone dead, and that the man was speaking to him in his own language. His accent was so perfect that, if Michael closed his eyes, he could imagine that the Director or one of the trainers was speaking. "I see that He was right, as He always is. You are wiser than you perhaps know."

"How do you know my language?" Michael demanded. "What kind of a trick is this?"

"It is no trick," the man said, limping around the desk. "It is a skill I have—temporarily—so that I can better communicate with you. And so that you can better communicate with me. He cares for us equally, you know. You no more than I, and I no more than you."

This, Michael thought, was gibberish, even if it was spoken in his own language. "Who is *he?*" Michael demanded, somehow dreading the answer.

"Ah," the Revelator said, placing a hand on his desk, "then it is true that your world has forgotten Him. But if you do not know who He is already, I am afraid I cannot tell you, at least not yet. But know that he is the true ruler of Mirrorvax, and I am only His servant. My name is Siwarth Cincura, as you know. You are wondering whether I am the supreme civic authority in Snowhold. I am not. You are asking yourself whether I manipulate some kind of fantastic machinery. I do not, at least not in the sense you suppose. You are wondering how I know you, how you were cured of your sickness, and why I can answer your questions even before you ask them. The answer is simple. I have the Authority, power from Him, to do so. You have a misunderstanding of what my Authority is, but you may learn more in time."

Michael stared at the Revelator in silence. It had been as if the man had plucked each of the questions from his mind just as it arose. Telepathy, he thought. It must have something to do with unfathomable mental powers. He chilled. "Why have you brought me here?" he asked. "What do you want from me?"

The Revelator moved to the front of his desk. "If you were the typical young man I meet in this office on drowsy afternoons, I would ask you if you were kind to your friends and relations and if you had read the Canons. Then I would tell you to continue to be kind and to begin reading the Canons." He paused, and his expression dimmed. "The questions I will ask you are similar, but they are far more serious."

"You seem to know everything about me. What more information can I give you?"

The Revelator licked his lips. "I do not need information. I hope only for your cooperation."

"Cooperation? How? To do what?" Michael tightened his lips. "You should know, since you seem to know everything else, that I am an asset of the Transvax Conglomerate of my world. I was hard-won by them. I would rather die than betray Transvax. If you want to use me against my world, kill me now; because I will not yield, no matter how you torment me—"

"Why would I want to torment you? Why would I force you to do anything you were not willing to do already?" The Revelator stared at him. "I would violate one of the highest laws He has given me if I did that. I would be stripped of my power if I tried to *force* you to do anything."

"Then what do you expect me to do?" Michael asked. He felt disarmed by the man; there seemed no logic or con-

sistency in what he said. Though Michael had been prepared to meet a technological wizard or a shrewd Mirrorvaxan chieftain, he had not expected this quiet-spoken old
man. The thought crossed his mind that the Revelator was
mad; but if so, he was brilliantly mad, given his mastery
of the Vaxan language and his mysterious knowledge about
Michael, himself.

The Revelator stared at him. "I would like you to go back
to your vessel and back to your planet. When you return
to your own people, I would like you to convince them not
to send other vessels here."

"That's absurd!" Michael said. The Revelator must know
less about Vax than he pretended, if this was his request.
What reason would Michael have for discouraging Transvax's conquest of this planet? And even if he wanted to
sway them, what power did he have to convince the Secretariat, or even the Director? "I could never persuade them
not to colonize this world," he said.

"Then you must stop them another way."

"But why would I want to stop them?"

"You must not let them come to Mirrorvax," the Revelator said. The lines deepened on his forehead. "Mirrorvax
is our world, and Vax is yours. He does not want your
people to come here, because they would make our people
slaves."

"Not slaves," Michael said, staring at him. "We will
make your people civilized. We will make your world clean
and efficient. Surely if you know who I am, you must understand that. And whether you like it or not, my people will
come. We will take your world."

The rims of the Revelator's eyes sparkled. "If your people come," he said in scarcely a whisper, "they will take
our world. They will make the stars fall in our skies, till
the oceans steam and the mountains flame. They will flood
Mirrorvax with fire, and when all is burned up that they
cannot use, they will level the forests and mine down the
mountains and raze our homes to make landing places for

166

your airships. They will not make my people civilized; they are not civilized themselves. They will kill our people and enslave them. They will bend our children and make them so they no longer know Him. They will make our world a second Vax."

"You don't understand," Michael said. But how, he thought, could a savage be expected to understand?

"If you bring other ships back," the Revelator went on, "we will resist you even less than you think. We have, in parts of our world, much more technology than you see here. But we have few weapons, and none that you do not already know about. Our strength is in Him and in His power. But His Authority does not turn aside the string of your death-machines. His Authority heals and mends and builds and connects. It never could be used to resist you. It never destroys."

Michael felt exhilaration where dread had been before; the Revelator, perhaps unwittingly, had told him the answer to his most important question. The Authority, presumably a body of psychic or superstitious power, could not be used as a weapon, no matter what other unusual capabilities it had. That this power had healed him, had enabled the Revelator to speak his language chilled him. But that the leader of the natives himself had admitted it was powerless against Vaxan technology made Michael take a deep breath. He would have a detailed and complete report to file to the Transvax Secretariat. He, far more than either Judy or Jeremy, would be able to outline the structure and weaknesses of the primitive Mirrorvaxan culture. A scientist, he was certain, would be able to explain this Authority and its manifestations. But Michael's information would be so powerful that the Director might appoint him to a crucial position in the planning or staging of the first wave of colonization, when the inevitable happened in a few short years. Michael clasped his hands together and smiled. For it was as if he held the fate of Mirrorvax captive between his palms.

MIRRORS OF COLOB

PERHAPS SENSING Michael's triumph, the Revelator turned
away. His limp seemed more pronounced and his posture
more bent as he moved to the wall behind his desk. Without looking back, he coiled a hand around a wooden knob
there and opened one of the panels like a door, inward to
darkness. "Michael," he said in an unsteady voice, "I would
like to show you something before you go."

"Show me something?" Michael said, tensing again.
"Why must you do that?"

For an answer, the Revelator turned his head. His eyes
no longer seemed silver, but gold instead, or perhaps even
crimson. Fire seemed to have rimmed them even though
he now stood in shadow, half his form eclipsed in darkness.
"Come," he said. The word was not a suggestion, nor was it
a command. When Michael moved toward the panel, he
was not sure it had even been spoken in his language or in
the Mirrorvaxan language. Perhaps it had not been spoken
at all.

Michael moved into the darkness. The Revelator followed
him, silently closing off all light behind them. Musty blackness—complete, cool, and thick—surrounded Michael, and
fear thrilled through him, for he could not remember hav-

ing ever experienced darkness so impenetrable and all-masking. But it was not like the lonely darkness that had made him cry out in the training complex, or the chilling, star-flecked darkness of space. Nor was it the kind of darkness that made him fear something was in it: a pitfall, a trap, or some death the Revelator had planned for him. Rather it made him fear that nothing was in it, and nothing beyond it. It was beginning darkness, as might clothe the inside of an egg or the shell of a seed pressed deep in soil. It was embryo darkness. It was the kind of darkness Michael imagined had been in the universe, billions upon billions of years before, before the first sparkle of light had appeared.

"Do not be afraid," the Revelator said. "Follow my voice."

Cautiously Michael walked after the sound of the Revelator's footsteps. They clicked faintly on a hard floor, just ahead of him. Their sound was like the rasp of beetles in a subterranean cave, or the flutter of moths' wings in starless darkness. But soon they hesitated, then halted. Michael stopped, too, staring blindly ahead of him. "Why have you brought me here?" he asked. "What do you want to show me? I demand an explanation!"

"Peace," the Revelator said. "Watch, and you will see."

Michael stared, but he saw nothing. He did not even see the specks his mind sometimes painted on darkness. He began to think that the Revelator was mad, or that even now the Revelator might be drawing a knife to kill him. He had almost decided to bolt for the door when something caught the corner of his eye. A spark. Like light from a burning speck of dust. Then another. Then a third, a little brighter, but still faint, as if indeterminably distant. Then more dots appeared, all around him, above him, and below him. Each light seemed brighter and closer than the one before, and soon Michael began noticing colors and patterns. These were stars, he realized, or representations of them, set in constellations as if this room were a simulator of space like the one at the Transvax training complex. It undoubtedly was something similar. The illusion was probably done with mirrors, for Michael could see nothing that might project it.

"The universe," the Revelator said, in a low voice. "As it was ages before our time."

Details now flickered among the stars; hazy patches of light—nebulae, shifting rings of stars, and comets or meteors that streaked pale lines through patches of darkness. Michael blinked, wondering if he had been hypnotized. For around some of the nearest stars he imagined planets circling. He could almost see some of them in his mind: gigantic gas planets brooding in the red light of huge suns; pale, ice-crusted worlds eclipsed in blackness; sallow moons leading shadows over the blue oceans of living worlds. And he began to imagine, as irrational as it was, that he could hear the universe around him, in insectlike clicks of radioactivity, and, more submerged, in a chatter like voices on a faint radio signal.

Then, just to his left, a bright star appeared, pulsing slightly. Tinted blue, it grew larger and brighter until Michael was not sure whether it was one star or many, or whether it had anything to do with stars at all. When he saw it, his mind abandoned all the other suns and their worlds. His attention focused, without his consent, on the bright mass. The severity of its light stung his eyes. He fancied he could feel the distant heat of its fires. But more, he felt something he could not explain, not in Vaxan vocabulary, and not even with terms he had come to know on Mirrorvax. The feeling the bright mass gave him was something like the feeling he had known when Anamandra had kissed him under the trees by the canal. But it was so much more intense, so much fiercer, wilder, and more painful that he could bear neither to look nor to look away. Something began burning deep within his chest, as if his veins had caught fire and were sending flame into his heart. Anguish and peace battled for a seat in his mind, but devastation took it instead—a feeling of emptiness, not from the star but from the sudden recognition that he did not understand its power. His hands relaxed to his side. His lips loosened. His mind, stripped of its last defense, began to pierce deeper into the cloud, to see burning shapes in it. He squeezed his eyes closed but still saw light, light falling like rain or arrows, light streaking across the universe, light touching planets, revealing them brightly, as if with lightning. A flash showed him Vax, then Mirrorvax; he seemed to see all that he had seen on both worlds, all the heaviness and order and misery of Vax placed beside all the calmness and order and happiness of Mirrorvax. He turned his head away, but saw only the cloud of stars again, hotter than it had been before, and so clear in its glittering majesty that he suddenly understood exactly what it was.

"Colob," he said, his voice sharp with hope and pain. "Colob!" Before he could cry the name a third time, the star began to fade, to dwindle like the tailfire of a rocket roaring away. It was almost gone by the time he whispered, "Colob."

The Revelator spoke, in a voice as cool as the darkness that came in the cloud's wake. "Yes, Michael. The light you saw represented Colob, the Great Star. You recognize it even though your race has for thousands of years tried to forget Colob, just as it has tried to forget Him. I have shown you Colob because you must understand our world and your own."

"Colob," Michael stammered. "Colob . . . is . . . home."

"Colob is no more than that, but it is no less. It is the source of both our peoples. It is where we came from. It is where we are going." The other stars were fading now, but the darkness replacing them was soft and comforting. "Thousands of years ago, ships of fire from Colob came to this solar system. A few isolated ships brought their passengers to this world; many, many others went to your world. Our races are brother-peoples, unalike only in superficial detail. The Canons have told us of your existence for as long as we have inhabited this world, though many of our race have forgotten you, and though your world, because it denied Him, forgot ours. But still, your world, like ours, is under His law. And His law says that your world will always be yours, no matter what you do with it; and our world must be ours. You cannot let your people take it from us."

"Would He intervene if we tried?" Michael asked.

"Colob itself would tremble, but bound by his own law, He would not interfere. He has saved His worlds before, but always through one of us. That is the only way he can work. That is why you must help us. If you do not, our people and our world will be destroyed, for all He can do."

"But you don't understand," Michael said. "You don't understand at all. We mean you no harm. We want only to make Mirrorvax better." But by some power of the Revelator, he glimpsed more of Mirrorvax, parts of the world he had not seen; he saw a great city on a peninsula, dominated by tall buildings, meshed with power lines, its streets filled with people. But it was not like a Vaxan city in spite of its size; he realized suddenly that Mirrorvax was both more and less like Vax than he had believed, and that if his ship had landed near the city, he would have met an Anamandra in its streets. "We mean you no harm!" he repeated. But suddenly his own words sounded hollow. He could not force from his mind pictures of short-barrels and air-shuttles and death-coils and barb-throwers; thoughts of Mirrorvaxan mountains burning, flashes of a demonic smile on the Director's face. Rage and anguish fountained up inside him, and he shouted, "We mean you no harm!" He imagined Anamandra running from her house, the sky raining fire behind her. "We mean you no harm!"

His last shell of restraint cracked, and he started in the direction of the panel door. Threads of light from beyond now revealed it. From the darkness behind, the Revelator called to him as he struggled to open it. "Michael! You must help us! You must see that your people let us live!"

The panel yawned open, and Michael plunged into bright afternoon sunlight. He collided with the Revelator's desk, then fumbled around it. He groped for the doorknob, then dashed onto the landing and down the steps. The Revelator did not call after him again, but the words he had said drummed in Michael's brain. Flights of steps raced by; he leaped down them, hardly touching them. When he reached the bottom floor, he burst out the front door, catching only a fleeting glimpse of Ratham and Anamandra's father before bolting across the lawn and through the gate into the street.

He had to run. Running was the only way he would be able to escape what the Revelator said. He ran to keep himself from listening. He ran to put a buffer of distance between him and the old man with the deep voice. He ran in the shadow of the temple, pushing people aside, weaving in and out among them, dodging wagons. The crowded streets frustrated him because they slowed his escape, but when his mind cleared somewhat, he realized the crowd might help him lose whatever pursuit the Revelator sent after him. When he had run two blocks beyond the temple, he glanced back. The wagon he had come to Snowhold in rested in front of the house, and there was no one in the part of the yard he could see. But that hardly meant he would not be hunted down. The Revelator, after all, knew Michael had the key to the destruction of Mirrorvax. The Revelator knew Michael was not willing to cooperate. They had no further use for him, then. They would kill him. He redoubled his effort and darted into a side street.

Out of the thickest crowd, he broke into a trot. Running was not easy in the spacesuit; he was already out of breath. Realizing he ought to save some of his energy for an emergency, he slowed his pace. Already, however, the buildings of Snowhold were thinning, and less than a block away was the river, here unbridged, flanked by sun-sparkled trees. After a moment's hesitation, he decided he would not look for a bridge; the Revelator might be able to guard the bridges easily. Hardly slowing down, he hurried across the bank, splashed through the shallows, pushed his way through the main current, then scrambled up the opposite bank, into the house-dotted farm country beyond. Fields and gates sped by as, trailing speckles of water, he followed a dusty lane toward the hills that separated Snowhold from Rush Valley. When he felt himself being watched by children in trees and old women on porches, he cut into an orchard that led toward the canyon mouth. There, in the cover of the trees, he at last settled into a walk.

He had almost reached the far end of the orchard before he recovered his breath. His run, though, seemed to have lost anyone the Revelator had sent after him. But he could not afford to take chances, and he could not tell what power the Revelator might use to stop him. It was clear that he must return to the ship at once. With what information he had, he must return to Vax. He must report to the Director what he had learned. What happened after that was not his responsibility.

He would not return to Mirrorvax, he decided, not even if the Director offered him an important position in the colonization effort. Mirrorvax, in spite of the advanced city he had seen, was not dangerous technologically; Mirrorvaxan technology made no weapons. But he had begun to realize the planet was perilous in another way, in a way he had not guarded against. Primitive Mirrorvaxan emotions and reactions, apparently, could happen even to superior beings such as himself. In spite of his new resolution to go back to the ship, to close the image of Colob from his mind, he sensed feelings awake and churning inside him. Dread of the Revelator sapped his strength. Fear pumped in the rapid beats of his heart. And something more quiet and terrible made him think of Anamandra. The picture of her family's farm being blasted away by a blind air-shuttle made him shudder, and the more it repeated itself in his mind, the more he hated both the Director and the Revelator. Both of them, he realized, wanted him to do what he

174

could not do. How could he deliver a report to the Director that would mean devastation to Anamandra's planet and possibly her own death? But since he was an asset of Transvax, how could he justify trying to make the mission fail? How could he even justify falsifying information or not telling all he knew, in the slim hope of staving off a Transvax invasion of this planet?

He had never felt so torn. He had not often been forced to make decisions; a person's life on Vax was clear-cut, neat, and decided more by the bid of a computer than anything else. But here on Mirrorvax, in the shade of alien trees, he had no computer. He had no commander or companion to advise him. The whole matter, devastating in either possibility, grinned at him from the blur of light Colob had burned across his mind. "Please," he said, beginning to stagger, "please." He spoke to no one, not even himself. He wanted nothing more than for his thoughts to die away, for the dreadful knot in his stomach to resolve itself and leave him in peace.

Breaking into a run when he reached the edge of the orchard, he started toward the canyon mouth, which was laid deep with shadow from the low afternoon sun. Sunlight swept fire into his eyes; blinded, he kept the hills in sight only by flinging up his arm. Even after he dipped into the shadows of the hills and set off up the canyon, keeping to the cover of the rocks, the light stung his eyes and painted the shadows of the canyon with Colob-shaped blotches of yellow. The ruts in the canyon beneath, however, seemed empty. The trees that sometimes hid the road began to bend in the breeze that poured down from the mountains, but no lanterns or torches appeared in the deeps as the sun set, and though Michael heard the hum of the wind and the mutter of water against the canyon walls, he did not hear hoofbeats or voices.

Snowhold appeared behind him for the last time when he paused on a stony hill, just before sunset. A few lights winked from the extremities of the valley, but more clustered in the mass of trees that was the town. And in the center, like a clear jewel, the temple glowed, lamplit and conspicuous. Michael only winced and turned away. He was glad when the valley at last faded away behind knobby hills and notched cliffs. And he was happy when darkness let him abandon some caution. He kept his eyes from the stars by watching the canyon beneath.

When he had crossed perhaps half of the hill country, he stopped in the hollow of a rock to rest. He dozed fitfully for perhaps an hour, then dragged himself up. The energy and nutritional tablets he took from the survival pack in his breast pocket gave him enough strength to keep up a lope along a smooth ridge that paralleled the road. The country was less rugged here, and more open. But he found himself stumbling; a rock caught his boot and spun him to the ground. The gash in the elbow of his suit hardly seemed serious, but the jolt of the fall added a limp to his run and made the moonlit trees pass by more slowly.

In the midst of this, Judy's voice came to him over his translator. He expected a simple report of the ship's condition, but he soon detected a new urgency in her voice. "We have just repelled another alien attack," she said. "There were more of them this time, and they might have used some new weapon against us if we had given them time. Jeremy and I have spent the last few hours collecting documentation on native technology. Our recent findings indicate that none of it is advanced, but because we are so ill-equipped to repulse native aggression, Jeremy has decided to return to Vax—soon. You must return, Michael, if you can. We assume from your signals to us that you are alive. But Jeremy now fears you must be captive. Since heat scans indicate that no large concentration of natives is now approaching us, I will make a foray in the direction of your flares. If I do not find you, or if you do not return to the ship before I do, we cannot help you further, and we warn you that we may return to Vax without you." Michael groped his way along as he listened to Judy repeat her message. He knew Jeremy; even now, all preparations would be made for launch, and neither of them would delay leaving. How could they justify waiting for him any longer?

He again broke into a run. The thought of being abandoned on Mirrorvax chilled him; he imagined himself staring at the empty rocket burn, watching steam rise from the ash. It would be little comfort to expect the appearance of the first colonization effort in five or ten years, for he would have no place to go. He could hardly return to Anamandra's farm, and any other people on Mirrorvax would eventually recognize him and turn him over to the Revelator, who would probably have him killed. But still something dragged at his steps, making him dread seeing Judy or the ship again. For the more he hurried, the more quickly the terrible decision would come upon him. Anxiety rose in him again, acid-tasting in his throat, and he felt the strength evaporate from his legs.

Before morning Rush Valley appeared, a pale stripe of lowland beneath the burning stars. When Michael left the last sagebrush behind, he realized he had struck almost the center of the valley, and that the Amudsar farm, as easily identifiable from the bellowing of the cows and the crow of cocks as it was from its dark patch of trees and buildings. The distant sounds, and the imagined creaks and voices from the house, made Michael halt. He sniffed the air. The familiar smells in the predawn chillness made him want both to skirt the farm and pass it more closely. For though he knew it would be dangerous to come near it, something told him he could not help it. Anamandra's face glowed in his mind, blurred now at its edges by the beginnings of forgetfulness, but all the more precious because it was fading. A fierce sensation, like a burning column of pain, told him that he must tell Anamandra good-bye.

He would never see her again, he realized. If he returned to Vax, he would not return to this planet. And if he did not return to Vax, he would be killed. Suddenly he wished he could convince Anamandra to return to Vax with him.

It seemed the only way to save her from the destruction that would come to this planet. The destruction that must come to her planet because he could never betray Transvax. But the notion withered almost as soon as it came to his mind; he could bring Anamandra to Vax only as a specimen. When he returned to the training center, Transvax scientists would claim her and make her an exhibit, or worse, hurt her to find the information they wanted. Perhaps they would even kill her. He squeezed his eyes shut to push back images of what they might do. No, Anamandra could not come back with him.

The farmhouse, its roof dark against the morning stars, soon loomed up. Michael found himself in a world of memory: the wind stirred the branches of the trees in the front lawn and played in the rows of vegetables just beyond the fence. The window under which he had slept stared at him. One of the dogs stirred on the porch. Traces of smells and touches of memory closed in; they made him back away from the house, back along the road toward the canals and toward the mountains where the ship lay. He could not face Anamandra, he decided. If he did, how could he tell what awful and savage emotions might blind him to his duty and keep him from doing what he must.

But before he had edged past the barn, a shape moved in the trees, then came out the gate into the moonlight. In a sudden burst of joy and fear, Michael saw that it was Anamandra. Her walk and the luster of starlight on her hair were unmistakable. Dressed in a robe whose sleeves stirred slightly in the wind, she walked toward him, tilting her head and peering into the darkness. "Maicyl?" she called out softly. "Maicyl? Is that you?"

He tried to turn around, perhaps to run again. But his voice betrayed itself, braying out his pent-up anxiety. "Anamandra!" he shouted. "Anamandra!"

She ran to him, and he caught her in his arms. Suddenly oblivious to everything else, he held her to him, felt her hair brush his cheek, and her breath touch his throat as she cried, "Maicyl! Maicyl! I've been so worried about you. I couldn't sleep. I had a dream that you came—that is why I was waiting in the trees for you. What has happened?" She pulled back from him and read the lines on his face. "Tell me what has happened!"

He released her slowly. Unhappiness welled up to blur his view of her. "I cannot tell you," he said. Awkwardness with her language and the look on her face made him hesitate. He fought the terror he felt suddenly as he thought of leaving her and gripped her hand. "Anamandra," he said. "Anamandra, I have to go."

Her hand went limp. "Go?" she said. "Where?"

"Home," he stammered. "To my own place. Anamandra—"

"For how long?"

"For always," he said, choking on the words. "For always."

"But why?" she exclaimed, plucking her hand away. The tears that brightened her eyes began to inch onto her cheeks. "Why?" she repeated. "Maicyl, I don't understand. Why must you go?"

Michael turned his head away and blinked back warmth in his own eyes. But Anamandra's beauty did not empty from his mind. Suddenly he felt he was no longer himself, no longer Michael 2112439–851, no longer Michael the advocate or Michael the debtor or Michael the astronaut. Instead he was a pale, blind creature who had never known light, who had been caged in darkness for an eon and then exposed too suddenly to full daylight. He was a child, too, a baby as helpless and illogical as Anamandra's small sister, a being powerless but towering with longing, gaping with needs, crying with hopelessness and hope. Suddenly he knew nothing beyond a single, piercing desire, a wish that flooded through him, breaking his last defenses away, splashing pain into his mind. He must explain to Anamandra. He must make her understand why he was going and what would happen because of it. In his anxiety he began to speak to her in his own language, his words at first rushed and apologetic, speaking of Vax and how he had been bought by Transvax for two thousand chronas, and how he had come to her world only in preparation for its ruin. She looked down as he spoke, and the tears continued to pour from her eyes. He spoke more rapidly, shouting to her that his people meant no harm to hers and that she should not blame him for what he did, because how could he do it any differently? Could she expect him to betray Transvax and the Space Operations Corporation and the Director simply because he had primitive emotions for Mirrorvax and especially for one of its inhabitants? Could she? Would she expect anything different from herself, if she were in his position? Could she blame him when he had no choice, when the cruelty of circumstance had forced him into a decision that would hurt him as much as it hurt her?

Finally she stopped him by putting fingers to his cheek. "Michael," she said in a soft voice, "Michael. I don't want you to be hurt. And I don't blame you for anything, not anything, because I love you, and I know that you love me."

Anamandra had spoken, as the Revelator had, in Vaxan. From the glitter in her eyes, he guessed that she did not even know she had done so. But her voice, the same kind of cool, even, compassionate voice the Revelator had used, disarmed him. The image of Colob's flame blinded him again, and in a sudden moment of brokenness and devastating loneliness, he silenced the screaming voice in his mind. He took Anamandra in his arms, then said, with perfect expression in her language, "I must go because I must see that the stars do not fall to destroy your world. I must go because I love your world—maybe only a little—but more because I love you."

"I understand," she said. "I understand. So we will never see one another again?"

"No," he said. He closed his eyes. "No."

"But how will I ever love the world again without you,

180

even if you save it? How will I know that you yourself are safe and happy?"

An odd calmness enveloped him, and he glanced at the sky, paled now by the first hints of morning. "I will be happy and safe," he whispered. "You will understand that I am when you watch the sky and see a single star fall, brighter than others you have seen. When you see the star, you must not cry any more."

"But Michael," she said. "Michael . . ."

He took himself gently from her hold and moved away. "I have to go, Anamandra," he said. Then he turned and walked, shattered in his peace, broken in his resolution, until he reached the canal. On the canal bridge he turned around to look over the pastures, toward where the farm was hidden in dusky morning, with the stars over it paling away in the sunrise. "Anamandra," he whispered. His voice lost itself in the Mirrorvaxan dawn. "Good-bye," he said.

He met Judy before going far into the hills. Carrying a short-barrel and wearing a frown, she hurried to him; she eyed first his battered space suit, then his face. It was as if she were not sure she recognized him. As they started on the trail that led deeper into the mountains, she demanded an account of where he had been. Dully he told her that since the day he had followed her, he had been a captive of the natives, and that he had only just escaped. More details, he told her, he would put into his report. The main thing they had to do now was reach the ship.

"Reach the ship," she returned vaguely. She watched morning light up the sky as they walked along. "That sounds like something you memorized from one of the Director's information packets."

He looked at the ground. "I have forgotten all I memorized," he said.

"Forgotten?" she said; hints of a sneer tightened her lips. "What would the Director say about that?"

"May the Director burn," he said.

She halted him with a hand on his shoulder. "What was that?"

He raised his head, then repeated, "May the Director burn." Scorn edged his voice, and anger made his hands tremble.

Judy's eyes went wide, and for the first time since he had known her, she reminded him of something besides an imperial princess. "You mean that," she said, in scarcely a whisper. "You mean that, don't you?"

There was no good in hiding his feelings now. "Yes," Michael said. He glared at the hills of Mirrorvax, which the new sun had turned green-gold. "I no longer belong to the Director."

He could not at first understand Judy's reaction. Her expression continued to be dominated by surprise, but something like a smile opened on her lips. "Michael," she said. "Michael." She patted his back, and they started along the trail again. Judy's smile persisted, but it was some time before she spoke. "Whatever happened to you changed you," she said. "I knew that from the first moment I saw you. But I wasn't sure how much you had changed." Michael did not look at her. She went on, "And now that you are Michael instead of the Director, there are a few things you should know. A few things it is now safe to let you know."

"Something I should know? About what?"

"About what's happening . . . and about why you are here. About why you were chosen."

Michael felt a chill. The world he discovered on Mirrorvax was all too quickly fading away like a dream, and the iron-clad reality of Vax was fast encircling him. But he reminded himself of his resolution, then said, "The truth?"

"You have always been told the truth," Judy said. "But you never heard the whole of it. Jeremy discovered the whole truth only days before we left Vax; and of course we didn't dare tell you, for fear it would make you even more loyal to the Director than you already were. The Director himself was probably ordered by the Secretariat not to tell you."

"First of all, you did fit Mark's suit, and you were an advocate and thus easy to train," Judy went on. "That much is true, but it was hardly enough to select you by itself. Also, the Director did not trust Jeremy and me. Both of us had been with Transvax long enough to see some of its faults. But we were the only tools the Director had—others were trained with us, but what they learned about Transvax they tried to use to increase their personal power within the organization. That frightened the Director and the Secretariat. Rebellion is easy enough to deal with. Those who rebel are terminated. But those who are ambitious . . ." Judy's voice faltered. "Mark wanted power. He often challenged the Director, though Jeremy and I warned him to be silent. He is silent now, along with the other astronauts the Director arranged to have killed. When Jeremy and I heard of the accident, we promised one another we would not meet the same fate. We did our best to convince the Director of our loyalty to Transvax, though what he had done to the other astronauts made us far more hateful and rebellious than anyone else in the Space Operations Corporation. Our act was at least convincing enough that the Director kept us on; he realized that anyone to whom he gave enough knowledge to be an astronaut would present some risk. He used us, but he did not trust us. Not completely. He would trust no one completely. Many people in Transvax think of rebellion. But most people's rebellion is harmless. I have talked with dozens of people who think the same things I think—but nearly all of them hope for little more than mild reform within the Conglomerate. Human beings don't act half as much as they think. And when they act, they act not because of what they know, but instead because of what they *feel*. The Director killed Mark and the others to end opposition to his wishes and ambitions that might destroy the structure at Transvax. But he cut his own throat. Mark's death made me stop thinking and start feeling. Mark's death made me agree with Jeremy, who had begun *feeling* rebellion when Transvax took out part of his voice box."

Michael bowed his head. "But, in spite of anything else you can say, what you told me on the AOT is true: I was chosen only to be the Director's puppet."

"Partly," Judy said. "But if the Director had wanted only a puppet, he could have found an easier one to manipulate. Have you ever wondered why he chose you in particular? That was what Jeremy found out just before lift-off. I don't know if I should tell you, even now. It may change how you feel—"

"Nothing can change that," Michael said. But already Judy's honesty was eroding the resolution in his mind. Judy, however, did not continue immediately, and only after they had sighted the hill where the AOT had landed did she go on.

"The Director wanted a careful choice for the third astronaut, so he used the Space Corporation computer to scan the world records of Vax to find those who fit the size requirements. The computer gave him somewhere from thirty to fifty million names. These he took to the only computer on Vax capable of handling such a volume of data—the Secretariat's super computer, the Central Office Logic Operations Bank—they call it something for short, but I can't remember just what. Anyway, he asked the computer to deliver the hundred names that most closely fit his requirements, as he had outlined them. But mysteriously, the computer delivered to him only one name. The computer operators were at a loss to explain why the computer had malfunctioned. The Director reran the program, but he got the same result. He was furious, and he went before the Secretariat to ask that the computer be overhauled. The Secretariat, however, refused; so the Director had the auction complex computer bid for the one name the Central Office Logic Operations Bank had given him—yours."

Michael sighed. "Then I was chosen through a computer's malfunction."

"Perhaps," Judy replied. "But the Central Office Logic Operations Bank makes few mistakes. The rumor Jeremy heard just before lift-off claimed that someone had tampered with the Director's program—"

"But who?" Michael said. "I have heard the super computer is strictly controlled. Only the Secretariat can change its programming."

Judy fretted with a strand of hair. "That is your answer. The Secretariat. Someone in the Secretariat arranged for you to be chosen."

"Someone in the Secretariat?" Michael said, shaken. "Who? And why?"

"We will never know who, and we can only guess why. But a guess may not be far from the mark. Obscure resource have been placed in high and important positions before—seemingly from computer errors, or by chance happenings. No one discusses such events. But everyone knows what has happened."

Dizzied, Michael remembered a boy in his resource suburb who had not been auctioned at all; he had been taken directly from the suburb by Medron guards. "His father was not capital," someone had said. "His father must be a powerful man in Medron." Michael had at the time found it hard to believe that anyone besides capital would have children, then quietly turn them over to a resource training suburb to be raised, keeping track of them in order to do anonymous favors for them later.

"The Secretariat," Michael whispered. "The Secretariat?"

Judy averted her eyes and nodded slowly. Michael's eyes began to sting. He thought of Anamandra's family, and of her parents. Suddenly he yearned to return to Vax—they were scheduled to meet with the Secretariat when they returned. He would recognize his father or mother then, he was sure. The look in the eyes would betray them. All he had to do was follow through with his mission, return *The*

Arm of Transvax to his world.

"Are you all right?" Judy asked, squinting at him.

He closed his hands together. "Yes," he said. Then, as if to reassure himself, "Yes."

They started up the hill, and after a few curves of the trail, Michael said in a louder voice, still unsteady with dread, "What will you and Jeremy do now? Will you let the Director's project succeed?"

Judy hesitated. "No," she said. "We won't." She glanced at him. "Michael, I think you suspected all along that we wanted this mission to fail."

"Yes," Michael said. He tried not to think of the Secretariat. "Jeremy notified the Medron air-shuttle of our launch, didn't he? And he jammed our contact with the ground, so the Flats could not warn us—"

"I jammed contact with the ground," Judy said. "The plan was ours, not his alone."

"But when I spoiled your plan by dodging those missiles, why didn't you carry your plan through? You had plenty of opportunities. Why didn't you send the *AOT* into the sun?"

Judy brushed back her hair. "We were wrong, Michael. During the first sleeping period, when you had left us, we decided we had been wrong. Destroying the ship would hurt Transvax, but it would do little good in the long run. And it would destroy the few of us who knew the truth about Transvax. So since then we have been preparing a new plan. We will soon be ready to begin, with your help."

"A new plan?" Michael said, sensing a change in Judy's voice. "What is this new plan?"

"Jeremy told me not to tell you. He will explain when we return."

"But I must know. What is your plan?" The old fear had all but dissolved, but a new fear, in ways more terrible than the first, clouded Michael's mind. He persisted with his question until Judy shrugged.

"Very well," she said. "But you must not let Jeremy

know I told you." She cleared her throat. "The Director was wrong. But he was intelligent, and in some ways he was right. He knew that Mirrorvax was the key to boundless power for whoever mastered it." She glared at Michael suddenly "But we can master it ourselves, Michael. With the weapons we have aboard the ship, we three can subdue this planet. And with the tools we have on board, we can begin to reshape it, into a New Vax of our own design."

"And what about the natives?" Michael said, horror-stricken. "What if they don't want a new order?"

"They cannot resist us," Judy said. "They are inferior to us. Jeremy and I have repulsed several attacks on our own. The natives are simple and simple-minded. They will soon learn to obey us, out of fear, even if they can't recognize our superiority. You spent time among them. You must know that. But we will not treat them badly, and in the end they will be grateful to us. Our cause, Michael, is just—"

He looked at her. "What is our cause?"

"To free Vax from monsters like Transvax," she answered. "It will take time to build up technology here, of course. It will not be easy. Perhaps we ourselves will never return to Vax; but our children will; or our grandchildren, along with those natives we have trained in our way of thinking—"

"But when you urged me through my translator to return to the ship, because of a native attack," Michael stammered, "I thought—"

"We repulsed every attack," Judy said. "We told you that we were in danger only in order to have you return to us quickly. In order for our plan to succeed, you must be here with us. You must not work against us. We need your help. Michael—"

"Military retribution against Vax and Transvax?" Michael said. "*That* is your goal?"

"Liberation is our goal," she said.

He swallowed the dryness in his throat. "How can you be sure that, even if your plan succeeds, if your great-great-grandchildren conquer Vax, that they will do any good? Freedom is something that is inside people. It comes from the inside out—you can't force it from the outside in. What you are planning is madness!"

Judy's eyes became fierce again. "Can you think of a better plan, Michael? Or are you against us, now that you know that your father—whom you never knew—is a member of the Secretariat?"

His eyes burned. He wanted to shout to her about Anamandra. But he glimpsed the short-barrel on her shoulder and steadied himself. He sighed. "I am with you," he said. "I am against the Director. Perhaps," he said, forcing his voice to stay even, "perhaps you are right, after all."

Judy laughed, long and pleasantly. "I am glad that you have learned the value of sound thinking, Michael. For a moment you frightened me."

He forced a smile. "I am sure Jeremy has the particulars worked out. I will look forward to hearing them." She started through a narrow place in the trees, but he touched her shoulder. "Let me carry your short-barrel for you," he said. "It must be getting heavy by now."

She cradled it in her arms, then handed it to him. Closing his fingers around the activation box, he placed it over his shoulder. Almost wordlessly, they continued to the top of the hill and into the clearing the AOT had made.

If he had not seen the bullet-shaped spacecraft gleaming in the center of it, he would never have recognized it as the same clearing. Though signs of the great burning remained obvious, the place was no longer a wasteland of ash. Mirrorvaxan plants seemed to be hardier than their Vaxan counterparts; near the edges of the burn, grass was growing, pale green shoots that the sun made translucent. Ferns spread over some of the charred logs, and in hollows of the ash grew a kind of flower that had filled Anamandra's mother's garden. Only near the ship, where bootprints had packed the earth, did no plants grow. Not far from the hatch was Jeremy, watching them approach.

At that moment, more than at any other in his life, Michael wanted time. He wanted time to gaze back over the mountains, perhaps to glimpse Anamandra's valley. Time to be with Jeremy and Judy before he must leave them. Time to examine the new prize he carried—like a burden and a treasure—somewhere deep inside. But time would give him only one chance, he knew. A few paces away from Jeremy, he raised the short-barrel with trembling hands. He activated the trigger.

The welcoming smile on Jeremy's face faded slowly. As Michael edged the weapon toward him, his hands went to his belt, where a pair of death-coils hung. "Drop them," Michael said, between his teeth. "Judy, I want you beside Jeremy. Unstrap your weapons. Slowly."

"Michael," Judy said, going red. "What's got into you? You can't be serious!"

"I can," he said. "Drop your weapons, both of you." The whine of the short-barrel almost obscured his voice. He edged around them, keeping them at bay with the short-barrel, until he was between them and the ship.

"Michael," Jeremy said evenly. "What do you hope to do?"

"He wants to take the ship back to Vax," Judy said when she had put down her venom-eggs. "I told him about the Secretariat, and now—"

Michael began backing toward the ship. "Each of you has a survival packet. That will sustain you until you can contact the natives." He blinked back a mental picture of Anamandra and her family; it stung him to think of them as merely the "natives." "They will help and care for you. I understand that now. I should have understood that before. They will care for you. They cared for me." He'll take the ship back to Vax by himself," Jeremy said. "He still belongs to the Director!"

"Michael, you're mad!" Judy cried out.

"I am taking the ship," Michael said. "I am sorry. But I have to—"

189

"Perhaps he *is* mad," Jeremy muttered to Judy. "But whether he is or not, I don't think he would hurt us." Jeremy took a step forward. Michael dipped the short-barrel toward the earth and slammed the trigger. Fire struck the ground just in front of Jeremy, vaporizing the weapons he and Judy had dropped there. A gash in the earth steamed as Jeremy backed away. Michael activated the weapon again; before Jeremy could move, it was ready to fire again.

"I advise you to put some distance between you and the ship," he said. He backed away from them and edged up the stairs into the airlock. His gloved hand paused on the lever that would close them out, himself in. He blinked at them; they washed away in the regret that brimmed in his eyes. "I'm sorry," he said. "Good luck to both of you."

He closed the door, then felt the elevator moving him toward the control cabin. When he looked up, fire replaced tears in his eyes. The ultimate choice waited for him, somewhere far above.

THE GIFT

ANAMANDRA BROUGHT her knee up against her as she squinted at the stars beyond the trees. They glittered there, like jewels scattered on a dark cloth or like the lights of a great city built on the wispy clouds. She had always considered stars beautiful, but now she knew they were also haunting. All day her early-morning encounter with Michael had seemed like a dream, and now that the night breeze made her shiver and the stars stared at her, still and unmoving, she began to wonder if it had indeed been a dream. The thought made her eyes sting again, made them dart to the pastures for perhaps a glimpse of him coming, even now. But no; she had not dreamed her meeting with him. If she had, her dreams had become tormentingly real.

A squeak behind her made her turn. The door opened, and her father emerged. He sat down beside her on the step and put his arm around her. "It is late," he said. "And it is getting cold. Do you want to come inside?"

"No," she said, averting her eyes. She had avoided talking to him since he had returned from Snowhold, even though Elissa, Corbi, and Aric had asked him dozens of questions about Michael. He had answered none of them, though; and his grim look had only added to her anxiety. "I would like to stay," she said.

He closed his eyes, then said softly, "He has circled heaven many times to build his courage. But it will not be long now."

She did not understand what he said, though she could tell by his tone of voice that he spoke with the Authority. He peered past her at the sky, then said, "Look, Anamandra."

She glanced up just in time to see a line of glittering light pass across the sky. Sparkling faintly blue, it swept fire across the mountains and seemed to brighten the sky. But soon it was gone, and the stars resumed their gentle twinkle.

In spite of what Michael had told her, she began to cry. Her father tightened his hold on her and whispered, as if he understood everything that she did and even more, "It is a gift, Anamandra, a gift freely given. It is one of the noblest gifts He has given us since He gave us the Authority. Anamandra, you must not forget that He has planned all of this, and nothing has happened that should not have happened. This was *meant* to happen."

"But doesn't love come from Him?" Anamandra said, blinking at him. "I know it does, and I can't believe He would make me love if He did not mean for me to go on loving!"

Her father answered only after the edge of the moon came over the mountains. "But of course you must go on loving, Anamandra," he said. "You must love him always. You can do no less."